The
KREUTZER
SONATA

The
KREUTZER
SONATA

a novel

MARGRIET DE MOOR

ARCADE PUBLISHING • NEW YORK

First published in 2001 in the Netherlands as *Kreutzersonate* by
Uitgeverij Contact

This translation published with the financial support of the
Foundation for the Production and Translation of Dutch literature.

This is a work of fiction. Names, places, characters, and incidents are
either the products of the author's imagination or are used fictitiously.

Arcade Publishing books may be purchased in bulk at special
discounts for sales promotion, corporate gifts, fund-raising, or
educational purposes. Special editions can also be created to
specifications. For details, contact the Special Sales Department,
Arcade Publishing, 307 West 36th Street, 11th Floor, New York, NY
10018 or arcade@skyhorsepublishing.com.

Arcade Publishing® is a registered trademark of Skyhorse Publishing,
Inc.®, a Delaware corporation.

Visit our website at www.arcadepub.com.

10 9 8 7 6 5 4 3 2 1

Library of Congress Cataloging-in-Publication Data is available on
file.

ISBN: 978-1-61145-864-0

Printed in the United States of America

Now, the duty of chastity is of a vast extent; is it their willingness that we would have women restrain?

I see no marriages where the conjugal intelligence sooner fails, than those that we contract upon the account of beauty and amorous desires; there should be a more solid and constant foundation, and they should proceed with greater circumspection; this furious ardor is worth nothing.

—Michel de Montaigne

en years later I met the blind music critic once again, the patrician-born Marius van Vlooten, who as a student had been so tormented by love that he put a bullet through his head. He was last in line at one of the check-in counters at Schiphol Airport, and I recognized him immediately by the aura of rage clinging to his tall, bent frame. His head gleamed. Wearing a navy blue raincoat despite the fine summer weather, he shuffled forward with the rest of the line, tapping his white cane. I remembered being surprised the last time at how awkwardly he explored the ground with his cane, as if in the initial phase of his blindness, in its infancy, he had neglected to train this special sense and learn the correct habits. I stepped in line behind him. As I assumed that he was also on his way to the Salzburg Festival, I decided to make myself known.

I coughed. "Mr. van Vlooten ..." I briefly laid

my fingers on his forearm. I hadn't forgotten that a voice and a touch are all a blind person needs to conjure up a figure from the distant past.

I told him my name. "You may not remember me, but we met —"

Turning abruptly in my direction, he silenced me with a wave of his hand. I looked straight into his face. With a shock, I saw how much it had changed and could hardly believe that time alone had done such damage. There were dark circles under his eyes, and a powerful muscle was tugging at the corner of his mouth. I was already familiar with the pitted scar the bullet had left above his ear, so instead of startling me, it merely evoked fleeting memories of summer evenings, of exquisite chandelier-lit meals, of the short canon for violin and cello with its C#–D–C#–B–C#–F#–D–C#–B motif: the circumstances of our first meeting.

"Of course I remember you!" he said, interrupting my aural vision, and I recognized his hoarse, haughty voice. "You're the young man who once kept me company on a flight to Bordeaux."

"That's right," I immediately agreed. "We had a long stopover in Brussels."

He stuck out his chin.

"Do I remember you — you and your kind!" His face turned red. "Intelligent, interested in too many things at once, and thus lacking in true passion. Graduate of the Institute of Musicology at the University of Amsterdam. Scholarship, part-time job, no money from home, a master's thesis on Schoenberg."

I nodded in spite of myself.

"A couple of short-lived affairs that you people refer to as 'relationships,' with women you refer to as 'girlfriends.' You eventually marry one of them, after having reasonably and logically explained to yourself why she's the perfect mate, then you take out a mortgage in both names. Just let me ask you this: What in God's name is the point of it all?"

The anger in his voice had risen to shameless heights. The people in line swiveled around to look. The irritation, the air of seething discontent, which I had noticed before and had unhesitatingly, compassionately, attributed to his youthful folly, had evidently turned to rage. I stared at him in silence until he turned away with a clearly audible growl. Without the slightest transition, as if I were engrossed in a book, I thought: What counts is not the deed itself, but how you deal with its consequences.

It was five-thirty in the afternoon. The August sun was streaming in through the windows of the departure lounge. The line slowly inched forward. Passengers were checking in not only for Salzburg but also for Bucharest, which meant long and hard negotiations about the oddest types of baggage. I had plenty of time to think about the drama that he, van

Vlooten, had referred to ten years ago as his "lovesick act of stupidity," the facts of which he had related to me in detail, without a trace of self-pity, when we had been stranded at the airport in Brussels.

It had been summer then as well. Summer is the season of music festivals, competitions, and master classes. I was on my way to Bordeaux, to attend a master class for string quartets at Château Mähler-Bresse. After a great deal of pleading, the organizers had managed to sign on Eugene Lehner, the former viola player of the legendary Kolisch Quartet. I was hoping for a chance to speak with him, between sessions, about a paper I was working on. That he was still alive and accessible seemed inconceivable. Not because of his age — he must have been nearly seventy then — but because he was the embodiment of a certain type of acuity, a certain auditory dedication, that belonged to a deep, dark, already vanished past.

Why I had decided to fly I no longer remember. I like to travel by train, even nowadays, because although the modern bullet train is a brash upstart — with a snack bar, armrests that don't flip up, and pursers who introduce themselves over the intercom by their first and last names, offer you their personal services in three languages, and then disappear for the rest of the trip — the stations are still wonderful. Domed roofs, semaphores, switches, the Salle d'Attente Première Classe, slowly vanishing from sight as you stare through the window of your compartment: a rocking, gently bouncing world of plush seats, from which travelers tell their life stories as they lean in closer to listen to each other, is almost yours for the asking.

When I boarded the plane to Brussels, van Vlooten was already sitting in the aisle seat, the one next to mine. I knew him, though not personally. He was — and still is — reputed to be a brilliant critic, absolutely independent, a man, for example, who could indicate with a few subtle strokes of his pen when the eccentricity in twentieth-century music is a mere pretext, an aim in itself, or the inevitable result of a person taking a stand. I wasn't surprised that he was flying economy class. It was general knowledge that he wished, for reasons of his own, to hide his material wealth from the world — a peculiar habit I had once heard compared to "an Eastern beauty covering her face with a veil."

I apologized. He stood up. I squeezed past him. The plane took off after a delay of only half an hour, which meant that I would be able to catch my connecting flight to Bordeaux. During the twenty-five minutes it took to reach Brussels, my seatmate and I ate a croissant and drank a cup of coffee. That was it. We struck up a conversation only after van Vlooten, despite his tapping cane, bumped into a marble pillar in the airport lounge in Brussels.

He stepped backward.

"Well, I'll be damned!"

I had come up right behind him, and took him by the arm.

"Are you hurt?"

The incident took place soon after we had been informed that the flight to Bordeaux had been delayed until further notice. What we didn't know then, but found out bit by bit as the afternoon wore on, was that the Boeing 737 that was supposed to take us to Bordeaux had crashed at Heathrow Airport, for reasons yet unknown, with a total of 150 passengers on board.

"Hurt? Humph! That pillar was about a foot and a half closer than it should have been. Anyway, why don't you join me? Let's go find the bar. The least I can do is offer you a Scotch."

I had no idea where the bar might be among the various counters and kiosks, but I helpfully took hold of his elbow. After a few short steps, I realized that he knew where he was going, so I surrendered to his excellent sense of direction. As he traversed the remainder of the departure lounge, he didn't say a word. He seemed to be holding his breath. Just as I was about to warn him with a squeeze of my hand that a large electric cart was parked in our path, he veered to the right. Only after we had safely passed the vehicle did he briefly tap it with his cane, apparently just checking, and sure enough, the thing was really there. I glanced at him out of the corner of my eye and noticed the look of satisfaction on his face, but it wasn't until much later that I understood the exact nature of his feat — when I learned of a special sense, a subtle system of perception, that certain blind people are capable of developing, which allows them to detect obstacles within a radius of about six feet, to sense any trees, lampposts, garbage cans, recycling containers, or bike racks that might be blocking their path and to hone in on them as stationary objects, as presences in the dark emitting a weak signal that normal human senses can't pick up, a delicate nighttime frequency that in theory can only be relied on to work in a noise-free environment, though even in a racket blind people have been known, during an emergency or in a moment of supreme willpower, to utilize that miraculous instrument, stretched across the skin of the forehead, nose, and cheeks like an acoustic web and triggering, by the merest of pressures, a sensation that used to be called "seeing," except that it utilizes the entire face rather than just the eyes.

We came to the red neon letters of Charley's Bar, and van Vlooten went back to walking the way I would always remember him: stumbling around like a wounded giant. I caught sight of an empty table over by the mirror along the wall. My friend meekly placed his fingertips on my shoulder and followed me to the chairs, from which we were not to emerge for quite some time. We started sipping our first glass of

Scotch, and heard the loudspeaker above our heads announce that our flight to Bordeaux was still delayed. At a certain moment I was staring rather shamelessly at van Vlooten's forehead, noting that his encounter with the pillar had been far from gentle, when he sensed my interest.

He laughed in annoyance. "Go ahead, take a good look at the proof of my stupidity!"

I felt myself blush. "I'm sorry."

I averted my gaze from the shiny bump swelling up over his right eyebrow. Our conversation soon turned to that other, previous act of stupidity in his life, and I found it impossible to keep my eyes from straying toward the whitish scar above his ear, which, by the way, I could only see by looking in the mirror.

*A*re you sure you want to hear this?"

She was three years older than he. A graduate student in anthropology — "Yes, the girl, her name was Ines, was the decisive type" — who informed him after their second or third date that their romance was going to be temporary, since the moment she got her master's degree she was going to start on her Ph.D., doing her fieldwork in the highlands of eastern Venezuela where the Yanomami Indians lived, a plan she had long conceived of as a strictly solo affair. "Thinking about her," van Vlooten said to me, "means picturing her," and he began to describe a window.

An arched window, a pale blue sash, and beyond that a municipal park on a wintry day. A motionless bird, its feathers white as snow, perched on a black branch, while Ines sat on the windowsill and rummaged anxiously through her bag because she thought she had forgotten her house key. She was getting

ready to leave. "Try your coat pocket," he said inno-
cently, and watched the scene without registering the
farewell motif being played out before his eyes. She
stood up and scanned the room. It was a large, comfortable room in student lodgings on the Rapenburg
in Leiden. Big man-sized armchairs, the maroon uphol-
stery faded and worn, a table covered with a yellow
oilcloth, that kind of thing — after all, he was twenty-
two years old. Up against the paneling was the bed
in which he and his ladylove had spent the night, in
which they had eaten breakfast, in which they had
awkwardly propped themselves up on their elbows
to read the newspaper he had snatched from the mat
after padding down two flights of stairs in his bathrobe
and slippers, never imagining for a moment that she,
upstairs, had already made her own plans for her life.
And now she was looking at him as though he had
never kissed her body from head to toe. She found
her coat, fished the key out of one of the pockets,
and yawned, long and noisily. Five seconds later —
"Good-bye, then!"— she was gone.

He had been studying law. Yes, just as his father
and grandfather had before him: one had become a
cabinet minister and the other, his grandfather, had
served as royal equerry to Queen Juliana. He, Marius,
had been a talented child, raised in the lap of luxury.
Like his parents, who had friends from all over the
world and traveled a lot, he spoke three foreign lan-

guages and felt at home in the theaters and concert halls of London, Paris, Vienna, and Berlin. Neither he nor his parents had ever doubted that he was bound to do something great. The fact that this abstract destiny required him to enroll in law school, in Leiden of course, with no regard to any hidden talents he might possess, seemed to him a reasonable, necessary, rather mysterious duty. He had been a student for two years without worrying about what the point of it might be. Then, one winter morning after a party, he discovered the central focus of his life. After a long rambling walk through the fog, Ines invited him in for a cup of coffee and a bacon omelet. Her dormitory lay on the edge of town, overlooking the fields. The elevator glided with hypnotic slowness to the top floor. Later that day, when he was home again, he sat down at the oilcloth-covered table, inserted a sheet of paper in his typewriter, and began to type: "The world . . ."

From that day on he longed for her face, her eyes, her gestures, the way she walked, the way she turned, the way she waited for him in her red coat at the back of the busy café where they had agreed to meet. She was nice to him. The reason he didn't notice the other source of tension in her — he was totally blind to the signs of her departure — was because of his passion.

Which, he thought, when he was by himself, he had under control. When he was alone, he believed that he was not thinking of Ines, but of the lecture notes on imperative and regulatory law, in a friend's neat handwriting, which he was copying for his own use. Yet as soon as he heard, at the appointed hour, the heavy downstairs door swing open and click back into the lock — Ines had a key to his lodgings — and heard her purposeful tread on the stairs, coming closer to him with every step, there was again nothing else and nothing more reassuring in the world than his passion, which, despite the fact that they saw each other almost every day, was growing more and more frenzied, you might even say neurotic, and which, he was quick to point out — and this was probably the most mystifying of all — she never failed to respond to. "And then a figure would appear on my doorstep, a vague female shape that had bicycled through the cold and was bundled in so many layers of clothes that she looked like a walking coatrack."

Van Vlooten fell silent.

"Yes?" I said.

"Just a moment."

The buzz of voices around us also died down. The loudspeaker above our heads began to hum, and I noticed that everyone in the now crowded bar was listening with serious, thoughtful expressions to the announcement that was ostensibly of interest only to us and to which we had long ago resigned ourselves. Once more, the flight to Bordeaux had been delayed.

The waiter brought us another Scotch. We took a

sip and sat in silence. I was convinced that van Vlooten could feel, just as I did, the throb of danger being discussed at every table in the bar. My eyes met those of a man folding up a Belgian newspaper. As if I had asked him a question, he rose, but when he reached our table, he plucked van Vlooten's sleeve.

"The landing gear jammed," he told my companion. "I heard that the pilot tried to land anyway."

And without waiting for our comments, he strode, briefcase in hand, out through the glass door.

Van Vlooten resumed his narrative, but I felt uneasy. I knew how it would end. With every word he spoke, I could feel the dark event drawing closer, and at the same time I could feel its presence hovering over me like a fait accompli. She started coming late. She started canceling their dates, hardly bothering to explain why. By then it was summertime, and she had begun to drop by his house in Wassenaar on the weekends. He and his parents might be waiting for her, sitting casually on the porch steps, early on a Sunday afternoon as the shadows of the chestnut trees crept toward the stables and there seemed to be all the time in the world. And then the phone would ring. How was it possible that none of this really bothered him?

I didn't reply. I hadn't asked him anything. I still remember my discomfort when suddenly, in midsentence, the face across from me stretched its muscles the way the blind often do in an attempt to reproduce a smile — a reflex from an earlier life. I didn't smile back. It was possible, he told me, because Ines continued to sleep with him, because Ines continued to play on his love, passionately, and with the greatest of personal interest.

His voice filled with sarcasm. "And what that meant, in those days, is something you young people can't even begin to imagine."

He twisted around in his chair and snapped his fingers. The waiter materialized instantly. "Sir?" Van Vlooten merely pointed two splayed fingers at the table and began explaining to me: "In those days a woman didn't go to bed with a man on a mere whim. Women had more pride, more basic instincts. Giving yourself to a man — that's how even the most promiscuous of them referred to their sexual favors, and even the most promiscuous of them recognized the hidden law at work in their bodies, which states that every organism is out to ensure the survival and advancement of its own genes: in other words, that she could get pregnant. Oh, yes, back in those days people still equated love with procreation, and I was no exception. I took it for granted that this beautiful woman would bear me five children!"

She graduated at the end of the following February. For one long month she had barely shown her face, but he assumed that her attention had been taken up entirely by her thesis. To him, it was still a time of love, and Ines was his entire world. They celebrated her farewell party in a former tram depot in Oegstgeest, which still housed two old-fashioned blue trams, their signs pointing eternally to OEGEE. About a hundred people came. Ines wore a strapless scarlet evening gown, and afterward rode home with him on the back of his motorcycle to his room on Rapenburg. There, in the early hours of the morning, they made love. "I'll call you," she said as she was leaving, after hours of blissful oblivion, when twilight was falling once more on the municipal gardens beyond the arched window.

He phoned her the next morning at about eleven, but there was no answer. Two hours later there was still no answer. After that he called every fifteen minutes, and when he finally reached her at ten past ten that evening, she was in such a hurry that all she could say was, "I'll call you back!" By 2:00 A.M. he was so tired of waiting that he raced full throttle to the dorm on the edge of town, only to find that her windows were dark, so he rang the bell and brought his mouth to the wretched intercom above the wretched row of mailboxes, but all was still. On the third day someone finally picked up the phone of the girl next door. A male voice told him jovially that Ines, whom he knew, had been driven to the airport that morning by a group of friends.

His mouth went dry.

Then he spit out one word: "Bastard!"

In those days Schiphol still seethed with dynamism and drama. Airline passengers, having been severed from their daily routine, maneuvered bags and suitcases through a fateful decor, where continents and capitals flickered before their eyes in phosphorescent letters, and they were filled with a new feeling about themselves. He didn't quite know what he was doing there. The flight to Caracas had left on time at 11:05. Now, up on the observation deck, he found himself scanning the runways, staring deep into the Haarlemmermeer polder. It was a gray day with a mournful wind that was impossible to see, because beneath those cloudy skies there wasn't a single tree on that entire stretch of land. He looked at the lifeless planes on the ground and thought of them as the souls of ships that had once sailed across Haarlem's stormy lake and anchored in this sheltered spot. He turned away. As he dialed the pay phone in the warm restaurant, his fingers felt dead.

This time the student next door answered immediately.

"Yes," the girl said. "This morning she —"

He interrupted.

"Tell me where I can find her in the wilderness. An address, a phone number. I'll take the next plane out."

The girl hesitated. "I'm sorry," she said, then delivered the final blow. Ines was not traveling alone, but with her boyfriend, a man who had just gotten a degree in Spanish literature, an amateur photographer. They had applied for a marriage license the day before yesterday and were planning to get married in Venezuela as soon as the required two-week waiting period was over.

Van Vlooten raised his arms as if he were lifting an intangible weight. "Interestingly enough," he said to me, "even as I held the phone, I could picture my father's revolver. I didn't have to think twice. Apparently the whole stupid plan was concocted on the spot."

A Smith & Wesson .22. Blue stainless steel. The weapon was kept in a case in the cabinet in his father's study. The cartridges were in a different drawer. He drove from Schiphol to Wassenaar at a calm, unhurried pace.

♪

Embarrassment. I suppose it was inevitable that my pleading eyes would fix themselves on his. But my silent entreaties failed to reach him and had no effect on the laconic tone of his voice or the blankness of his expression. Out of shame, or perhaps a need to be discreet, I averted my gaze from the face that had long been unaccustomed to reacting to other faces.

A completely irrelevant thought flashed through my mind: Had I or had I not remembered to put the old 1945 score in my suitcase? A glance in the mirror told me that the bar was now almost empty. A couple of card-playing men, a child, a redheaded woman engrossed in a book, and, much closer, the horrifyingly contorted profile of a man sitting with his back to a round clock and talking about something in great anger.

His mother had been home at the time. She was sitting at her desk in a side room, with the door open. She looked up, saw him head toward the stairs. A son come to fetch something. But he quickly stepped inside, took her hand, and kissed her fingertips. His father's study was upstairs, the corner room on the second floor. He nodded to the maid in the hall. A moment later, with no thought of death, he stared at the revolver, put the heavy object in his pocket, and took the cartridges. He drove through Voorschoten to his room in Leiden. Despite the anxiety of the last few days, it was neat and tidy. The hardwood floor creaked. He removed his cap and goggles, briefly rubbed his eyes, and loaded the gun. The idea of writing a farewell note never occurred to him; his heart was filled with just one goal. Facing away from the arched window, he released the safety catch and put the barrel to his head, just above his ear. "Maybe I pointed the thing a bit too far back," van Vlooten said to me. "Or else my aim was a bit crooked."

I looked at him. His head wobbled, as it had a moment ago, and that was all that could possibly be construed as emotion.

"Or else my aim was a bit crooked," he mumbled.

He drew a breath, but before he could go on, he was interrupted by the voice from the loudspeaker. The passengers for Flight AP 401 were requested to proceed to the gate as quickly as possible.

3

he bullet?" he finally said. "You want to know how someone can survive a bullet like that?"

He wiped his mouth and spread his napkin over the empty cups and plates.

"It happens more often than you think. Lots of cases have been reported. It won't surprise you to learn that most of them occur in Scandinavia."

We found ourselves in the chummy position of air passengers who have just consumed a rather decent, or actually a surprisingly good, meal. The French airlines, in those days still practicing the art of making amends, had served a 1970 Château Lalande along with the guinea fowl. I had the impression that both my seatmate and I, having reached the bottom of our glasses, had encountered a drink of the strongest kind, one with the character of an unreal, crystal-clear vision. The bullet, van Vlooten told me, had entered the posterior lobe of his cerebrum.

Leiden University Medical Center was known throughout the world, even in those days, for its neurotrauma unit. They brought him in through the entrance on Rijnsburgerweg, unconscious but alive. During the four-hour operation, in which they managed to stop the hemorrhaging and remove the blood clots, they found that the tissue of the cerebral cortex had been irreparably damaged in several places. Night had fallen by the time he regained consciousness, and he understood nothing of what was going on. Incredible exhaustion, voices, fingers fumbling at his arm — he asked the usual "Where am I?" then wanted to know the time. In the hours that followed, it slowly began to dawn on him that he had survived his death.

"Isn't the end of something always the beginning of something else?" van Vlooten inquired in a dramatic tone of voice.

His love for Ines ended at the same time his blindness began, so it's only logical that he looked upon love and blindness as the reciprocal poles of fate. Of course he was miserable to start with. Anguish, despair — inevitable when the light has gone out of your eyes from one moment to the next. "Wherever I found myself, there was no one but me. The person I thought of as 'me' lived inside a black bell jar. In the meantime, the rest of the world drifted away. After all, the world is something that has to be perceived; that's one of its most salient features. Your hands, nose, and mouth are effective enough when it comes to things that are near, but for distance you really need your eyes. I dreamed a lot. There were no sounds in my dreams, just a tantalizing mass of images that disappeared the moment I opened my eyes. If I then ran my hand over my scalp, I could feel the stubble growing back. And that was all. The sum total of my universe consisted of my body and the sheets on which I lay. In the end it was not curiosity, but sickening fear, that drove me out of bed to explore the dimensions of my room, to grope the walls and corners with my outstretched arms."

It was rainy that spring. On the porch of his parents' house, he sat in a rocking chair with his feet hooked over the rung. He was surrounded by ghostly apparitions: his parents, his sister Emily, friends, servants. They tiptoed around him, lowered their voices, anticipated his wishes long before he knew he had them. Go away, all of you, he thought. My arms hurt. My knees ache. What do you and I still have in common? Once upon a time I could figure out how fast I was walking by counting the trees.

At this point a new thought apparently occurred to van Vlooten. After a moment of silence, he turned to me.

"Do you also think that personal happiness, no matter how big or small, is determined by character rather than by external circumstances?" he asked.

Before I could reply, the purser appeared in the aisle with the beverage cart. He asked if we would like a glass of cognac, or perhaps Armagnac. In the dusky light, I watched van Vlooten as he held the glass under his nose. He's right, I thought. Yet even in the way he swirls the liquid in his glass, there's a hint of irritation.

But his voice remained calm. He adjusted his seatback, so I adjusted mine too. For some reason I sensed that coming events would take a favorable turn. At any rate, I think I had already suggested that it wasn't just the eyes, but also the ears that act as a powerful mediator between you and the firmament, between you and all the dominions of the earth, and that — He interrupted with a cough. "As I was saying, it was rainy that spring."

Cold, windy. From his rocking chair he heard the rain dripping on the newly unfurled leaves of the chestnut trees and, softer but more rhythmically, on the row of birches running down the drive, past the garage, and ending at the grassy slope where his mother's fat blond Shetland grazed. At night in bed he heard the wind come up and the storms get wilder. He could easily follow the perspective formed by the sloping roof, the perpendicular wall, the recessed doorway, the doorstep from which the water spattered, then on to the steady drip on the lawns and paths, and all the way over to the traffic on the N-44, where the cars swished back and forth between Amsterdam and

The Hague. In the early-morning silence he could hear the hedgehogs emerge from the bushes and scurry over to the kitchen to drink the cats' milk.

One day, around noon, he heard an airplane high in the sky. The drone came closer but also moved behind him and to the side, up and down, until it and its pounding vibrations seemed to fill the entire sky. As if he were peering at an atlas, he saw the territory over which the aircraft was flying; as if he were reading an in-flight magazine, he saw the dotted lines leaping like the rays of a rocket toward destinations everywhere: Paris, Vienna, Berlin, Zurich. . . . And at that moment his other life began.

Because what struck him then were not the parks and hotels he had once visited with his parents, nor the art museums, but — with an unbearable longing — the Salle Pleyel, the Musikverein, the Philharmonie, the Musikhalle. That night he waited until everyone else in the house had gone to bed before playing *The Rite of Spring* on the record player in the drawing room. It was a 1946 recording with Pierre Monteux and the San Francisco Symphony Orchestra, an old set of 78s, and God alone witnessed the concentration with which he placed the ten records on the turntable, flipped them over, and played the other side, and the pleasant shock with which he listened to the composition as it crackled and hummed beneath the rapidly revolving needle.

"In retrospect, a remarkably good recording," van Vlooten said to me. "Not without errors, but good heavens, if you were to ask me which orchestra has managed to produce such a sensual interpretation of that ingenious rhythm, that wicked tempo, that unforgivable delight in the girl's sacrifice . . ." The rest was lost in a sigh of contemplation.

Shortly afterward he wrote his first review, when the daily *Het Vaderland* sent him to the Diligentia Theater in The Hague to attend a performance by the Deller Consort. His sister Emily went with him. "She's pretty much of a bore these days," van Vlooten said, "but back then she was a fun-loving, giggly schoolgirl, educated at a boarding school in Brussels." When the countertenor began to sing a Purcell song, and every word of the lyrics, based on the opening lines of a Shakespeare play, could be understood clearly, she placed her hand on her brother's hand, with the best of intentions, mind you, but despite her good intentions it was horribly wrong, because he felt it had been motivated by a tenderheartedness that enabled her to see his enchantment without realizing that it didn't stem from his broken heart, but from an inexplicable emotion that was far beyond even his comprehension: *"If music be the food of love, come on come on, come on come on, till I am filled with joy!"*

♪

It marked the beginning of a life of cabs, trains, and planes, all culminating in an aisle seat in a concert hall. At first he took notes, jotting down key words that were later read aloud to him by his family, or when he was staying in a hotel, by an earnestly intoning chambermaid. Before long, however, his memory preferred to do away with this stimulus, and his themes and ideas would come tumbling out of the silence at such a speed that his typewriter couldn't always keep up, so that he would phone his editors and dictate his press-ready copy to them directly. He claimed that Chopin was a classicist, that during the four minutes of "La Lugubre Gondola" Liszt had entered a stranger world than Wagner ever had in his entire *Ring*, and he pointed out that Alban Berg, in one of his string quartets, used an A–B–H–F motif to link his initials with those of his secret love — a revelation thought at the time to be "groundless," but which later turned out to be true: his beloved was named Hanna Fuchs. Thanks to his financial independence, he could write about whatever he pleased, which meant that the *New York Times* would print his vigorous defense of Matthijs Vermeulen's Second Symphony one day —"furious, pounding, the Dutch *Sacre*"— and the next day the local *Zeeuwsche Courant* would get an extensive commentary on the Vienna State Opera's performance of *Lulu*.

To be a critic is to be an advocate. Van Vlooten

advocated the music of the era he lived in because it was most in need of his services, but in his heart he made no distinction between then and now. He used an old argument to champion the latest, starkest, aloofest of Stravinsky's works, *Threni*, maintaining that for the entire length of the piece the listener must believe in God. Then again, he wrote that there are pianists — a few here and there — who are able to make Beethoven and Schubert sound like the avantgarde composers they really were, pianists whose interpretations transform us into contemporaries of these masters and enable us to hear things we've never heard before.

From time to time van Vlooten expounded on the subject of music's flaunting of time. In the *Frankfurter Allgemeine Zeitung* he once reviewed the work of the Russian Galina Ustvolskaya, a genius who remained unknown for decades, even after he had heaped her with lofty praise. He had come across her work in Leningrad. Ustvolskaya was a recluse who lived in a tiny apartment in one of the city's massive suburbs. An embassy car had delivered him to her doorstep. Sometimes the deference accorded a physical handicap works to your advantage: the shy and retiring composer took his card, printed in German, let him in, and gave him tea. Within the hour, she and a cellist friend of hers were playing him the *Grand Duet for*

Cello and Piano. He was bowled over. At some point in his somewhat long, rather overenthusiastic article, he couldn't resist bringing up God again, this time claiming that the Almighty loved music, but not the visual arts. Perhaps van Vlooten, raised as an agnostic, sought consolation for his blindness. At any rate he wrote, "God often appears in the guise of time, so His appreciation of mankind's tinkering with time, i.e. music, is perfectly logical, while images, which bring time to a standstill, merely kindle His wrath."

He never got used to traveling in the darkness. Not being able to consult clocks in public places was a continual source of inconvenience. Yet he never let himself be deterred by a geographical location: If a program aroused his interest, he went, no matter where it was. This summer was the third time a master class for string quartets was being held in Bordeaux, with two public concerts at the end.

Van Vlooten leaned toward me. "Have you ever been before?"

I shook my head. "No."

"Me neither."

What was it about this rather modest event that appealed to him? I wondered. The young string quartets from all over the world?

"A Dutch quartet was also chosen to participate," I said.

"I know. The Schulhoff Quartet." His hand glided over the table, and he placed his glass in the circular indentation designed to hold it.

The passengers in front and to the side of us had switched off their reading lights. It was dim on board, and very quiet. There was only the drone of the plane, which seemed to have absorbed van Vlooten's story. He looked positively cheerful now, merely shifting in his seat every now and again to accommodate his large frame.

"The set pieces are nice," he said. "Haydn's Opus 103, Verdi's Quartet, Webern's *Bagatelles*."

"And Janáček. The first quartet, the repertoire piece that everyone plays, which is of course what makes it so difficult —"

"Ah, the *Kreutzer* Sonata!" He lifted his hands and picked up his glass again, but it was empty. "Shall we order another one?"

♪

And so we traveled that long-ago night from Brussels to Bordeaux. The flight couldn't have lasted more than an hour and a half, but when I think about it now, that seems ridiculous, since we not only argued about Janáček's first string quartet and exchanged life stories but also drifted off more than once into a deep sleep. As I recall, we ran into quite a bit of turbulence on the flight, and van Vlooten slept through the bumps with no more change in his breathing than that of a man turning over in his sleep. Yet at the same time, in the way of all memories and dreams, I hear our voices touching on the problematic theme of love.

"You asked if I'm married?" I heard him say. I didn't reply. He paused, then informed me that he had never fallen in love again. I said something about sexual desire. He waved my question away. Ah, women . . . Of course there were women! He was eternally grateful to them for their perfume and their softness and all manner of things. "Women are generous," he told me. "They naturally tend to fuss over the male of the species and turn his weaknesses into strengths. By pretending that they don't care, personally, whether the man in their life is blind as a bat, they do a lot for your self-esteem." Gratitude and affection, then, but no fire. And especially not the hot blaze of possessiveness or the fierce pangs of jealousy, neither of which he ever felt. And when his lady friends suggested that it was time to move on? No problem, he walked them to the door and waved good-bye to their fading footsteps.

Van Vlooten turned his head to the window and wondered aloud why it was so damned impossible to fall in love with a woman who was faceless.

"Oh, young man of sight," he said to me. "You're used to feeling an immediate shock when you see an attractive woman. You have no idea how peculiar it is to have to satisfy your erotic appetites without a visual image. You're probably thinking: Well, what about the other senses? No, a man who's reached adulthood with his sight intact is used to letting his eyes take precedence over his other senses."

I said nothing, merely drummed my fingers reflectively on the tabletop.

Then I asked him if in that case he might not be able to imagine the faces of his mistresses.

No.

Silence. He shifted in his seat. He explained that Ines had ruined him for life. Not because he mourned her loss — not at all, he had already told me that — but because it was *her* face, frozen in a smile, that he had envisioned as the female portrait to end all female portraits the moment he pulled the trigger.

"How dreadful," I said softly, then mumbled, with a cognac-induced eye to the interconnectedness of things, a line of Ovid that I remembered from my schooldays: "The poet received her and at the same time accepted this condition, that he must not turn his eyes behind him until he had emerged from the vale of Avernus." Alas! Suddenly saddened, I thought of the hapless Orpheus, who couldn't help casting a backward glance at his eternal love. Oh, for one quick look! At that very instant, however, the fog swallowed her up, and she sank out of sight with nary a reproach to her husband, who let her die a second death. "Farewell," she called modestly, and left it at that.

With my heart turning to ice, I began to think about the ineradicable smile of the two-timing Ines, and at a certain moment I even thought venomously, Go to hell.

"Would you like to know what she looked like?"

Van Vlooten. His voice sounded oddly muffled. Was he haunted by the line of verse I had quoted? Was he drunk with sleep? I could feel the plane beginning its descent.

She had observant eyes, the color of gooseberries, full lips, a strong, pale, heart-shaped face, and ash-blond hair. Apart from dark red lipstick, she used very little makeup. She was of average height, about five foot six, with rounded shoulders, which somehow suggested she had a caring nature and also helped to minimize her ample breasts. She had relatively long legs, and feet with high arches.

We lapsed into silence. The plane landed in the dark of night. Nearly a week went by before I saw van Vlooten again at Château Mähler-Bresse.

*L*ight catlike eyes," I said to him. "When she looks at you, you have the feeling she's mocking you, but in a friendly and relaxed way. Her mouth is small and symmetrical; her upper and lower lips are equally full. She has what I would call hazel hair, which, as I was surprised to note this week, comes to her waist when she wears it down, though today it's gathered into a braid at the back of her neck. It helps to accentuate the delicate line of her jaw, as well as her nose."

We were seated in the lounge of Château Mähler-Bresse. Van Vlooten's interested gaze was fixed on a tall palm tree in a copper pot, while I was looking a few feet to the right, where Suzanna Flier was actually sitting, talking to a young man with blond hair and nodding her head as she always did when she was enthusiastic. Had van Vlooten asked me to describe her? I don't recall. I had introduced her to him when

he turned up at the hotel earlier in the afternoon, at
the hour when the master-class students were beginning to join the hotel guests to view the vineyards
from the terrace or through the open French doors,
the sun already lower in the sky. He had stuck out his
hand, and she had placed her hand in his. Then they
exchanged a few polite remarks, standing beside the
swinging doors, where there was a lot of coming and
going and where four Scots, members of the Anonymous Quartet, whisked her away when she wheeled
around to see who had tapped her on the shoulder.

I had known Suzanna Flier since we were students, yet until this moment, when I was forced to
believe the evidence of my own ears, I had never
realized that she was extraordinarily beautiful.

She was the first violinist, and a good one at that,
in the Schulhoff Quartet. Suzanna Flier had been
blessed with one of those miraculous talents that people
are at a loss to explain, other than to say that it must be
a cosmic gift. She had been born to a working-class
family in Rijswijk. One day her father, a bus driver in
The Hague, must have taken his five-year-old daughter
and ridden in a coworker's bus all the way to the music
school on Prinsengracht, in the heart of The Hague,
and gotten out at the green gate where he himself had
stopped many times before. I had met him more than
once: an introverted man, thin, with black sideburns.
The intervening years had left him a widower. He

once came to the concert hall in the Royal Conservatory of Music dressed in his Sunday best to hear his daughter play Webern's *Five Movements.*

She and I never actually dared to have an affair. We were good friends for a while, so if I didn't feel like going back to Amsterdam at night, she would let me sleep in her one-room apartment on Lissabonsteeg. I could therefore have told van Vlooten, had he asked, that Suzanna Flier slept heavily, talked in her sleep, had a naturally sweet smell, and didn't diet — at least not in the mornings, when she would wolf down a breakfast of fresh poppy-seed rolls and cream puffs, fetched from the bakery by an attentive guest. Why the relationship never progressed any further, I no longer remember. I think she was the one who held back. Perhaps she was secretly having an affair with one of her professors, or sleeping with a budding composer or poet, because in those days the girls at the conservatory, unlike their sisters at the University of Amsterdam, did allow themselves such lapses.

To me, an undergraduate at the Institute of Musicology, The Hague was a far cry from Amsterdam. As I shuttled back and forth through the farmlands between one train station and another, my social circumstances underwent a complete metamorphosis. Roughly speaking, Amsterdam was busy casting off the chains of matrimony, while The Hague was quietly undermining symphony orchestras. At the Institute of

Musicology on Keizersgracht we male students and professors were supposed to take it in stride whenever the urinals had been cordoned off with ribbon. On the street, especially in Damrak and Leidseplein, we were subjected to female stares and whistles. You had to learn to put up with it. Walking alone past an outdoor café, where the women stood around in groups and drank, was sometimes a risky business. They poked each other, giggled, and stared brazenly at your fly, which was mildly embarrassing, if not downright irritating. In those days there was no pressure to graduate quickly. Conspiring female students, demonstrating against marriage as a form of slavery, didn't worry about things like grades, but demanded free birth-control pills. Naturally it was better, from a political point of view, not to go to bed with us oppressors at all. Amsterdam became lesbian, turning into a feminist bulwark that managed to get an entire generation of men to stop putting women on a pedestal and helping them into their coats.

Meanwhile, back in The Hague they were playing Schoenberg.

It was in this gray city by the sea that the lively, colorful ensembles sprang up that were to inspire the future world of Dutch music. Every time I entered the dilapidated conservatory on Beestenmarkt, I would find the students sitting stiffly and quaintly on the benches lining the walls of a bare room they called the "waiting room," with a frenzied cacophony all around. The teaching rooms in the nineteenth-century building weren't soundproof. They had creaking floors, superb grand pianos, cupboards jammed with scores, and enormous potbellied stoves stoked by a squat, uniformed custodian with ruddy cheeks they called Torchy, who devoted his life to keeping the fires burning. There was a concert hall on the third floor, where the waiting-room habitués were transformed into singers and instrumentalists who performed, with unbelievable dedication, works that had never before been heard in this country. I was always pleased that I had taken the trouble to come, because *seeing* music being played is of course very different from merely hearing it. I still remember watching in amazement as those students, spurred on by the music, threw themselves into a relationship of flagrant, deliberately controlled frenzy that dissolved moments later into something casual and indefinable.

"Oh, well," Suzanna Flier said to me one afternoon at the end of a rehearsal, when I had tagged along with her and the rest of the group to the harbor in Scheveningen. "I think I'll just have a herring."

The sea had been green, dark green, I thought as I walked into the busy lounge with van Vlooten trailing behind me. We had sat on the basalt rocks of the breakwater, watching the fishing boats go by. What made this memory now, all of a sudden, so vivid?

Suzanna Flier had pointed to the cabin of one of the ships, where a woman had looked up in our direction through the tiny square of the window, then smiled and waved because she thought we were waving at her.

"Oh, I could easily live that kind of life!" Suzanna Flier had said, a bit breathlessly. She had been so much fun, I remembered after van Vlooten and I had lowered ourselves into a couple of armchairs and I had started, on God knows what impulse, to describe to the blind man the young woman to whom I had just introduced him.

♪

He nodded, but said nothing. Yet I could tell I had sparked his interest. Or rather, that she had. Although he was paying attention, he began to twist his torso in that characteristic way of his, and when he raised his hand, a waiter once again sped to his side. While he leisurely inquired about the brands of Scotch they served, I continued to observe the violinist as she sat in the shaft of light slanting through the French doors, and I have to admit that the feeling that I was doing it for him, van Vlooten, was accompanied by no small enthusiasm of my own. He must feel like an outsider every time he meets someone, I thought, while casually noting that her thin yellow dress was cut low in the back and that her braid was resting against her pale skin.

At some point Suzanna Flier must have sensed the look of concentration being focused on her from across the room. She turned around, met my eyes, and in the same glance also took in the sumptuously furnished tableau of the waiter and the blind critic. Come join us, I beckoned wordlessly, and she smiled and inclined her head with her eyes closed, Okay, I'll be right over.

"What else?" van Vlooten urged, after placing his order.

Keeping my eyes on Suzanna Flier as she stood up and shook hands with the young blond man, who leapt to his feet, I went on painting her portrait, oil on canvas, and to this day I'm still amazed at the Picassoesque spirit that must have inspired me late that afternoon on a vineyard estate outside Bordeaux. If he wants to, I said to myself, he can mentally hang this picture on a wall or over a fireplace. She came directly toward us, giving us a full-face view: I described her straight shoulders, her corn-yellow sundress. She looked at us the way a person does from across a room, her facial expression arranging itself for the conversation to come: I sketched her smile, which was openhearted, yet also betrayed her tendency to tease. Three women crossed her path as they headed for the terrace, and she stepped aside and waited by a pillar. Narrowing my eyes, I meticulously described her creamy white neck, then enjoyed making the link between the creamy white arms of the girl before me and those of the violinist onstage, moving her bow up and down in her strapless, or at any rate sleeveless, gown, embracing the music she played, powerfully, fluidly, tenderly, broadly, or with just the merest tip, thus bringing the music physically close to the listener, as every concertgoer knows. Ah, there she was. Suzanna Flier loomed up a few feet away from our table, and I had just enough time to describe a bit of the background.

The drooping, serrated sword of a dark green palm leaf.

*A*ll of this took place amid a dazzling land-scape.

I too had gone out on the terrace to view the hills of Saint-Croix-du-Mont across from us. The rays of the sinking sun seemed to fill them with an inner glow. It was nearly seven o'clock. In the dusky lounge behind me, Marius van Vlooten and Suzanna Flier were deep in conversation. They had started off with the usual banalities. Was she enjoying herself? Yes, she was. Did she often take part in such week-long master classes? This was the first time. Was she pleased with the lessons of the Hungarian maestro, Eugene Lehner? She stared at him in silence, and I knew it was because she couldn't find the words to express her feelings.

"Those few hours . . . ," she began, then stopped again.

"Yes?" he prompted. "Those few hours?"

"They come from another world," she said with a bashful sigh.

They were sitting close together. Suzanna Flier, with her feminine intuition, had quickly realized that the blind man had to be able to touch her, to breathe in her presence. She was seated on a straight-backed chair that was somewhat higher than his, so she had to bend over to hear what he was saying. He in turn had cocked his big balding head in her direction, so that his face, with its quizzical expression, was pointed toward the terrace. They were both smoking. Every once in a while Suzanna Flier would look off to the side as she talked, so that when I turned around, I had the feeling that they were staring at me in complete unity.

In reality there was no unity. A week of master classes brings the participants close together. While van Vlooten had stayed with old family friends in Château Belvès in the Périgord, we had spent five intense days in each other's company. The master classes were held in a separate wing of the château. Although both students and teachers could retreat to their spacious rooms with baths, they were constantly running into each other in the hallways during the day and at the oddest hours of the night, if only to exchange parts or scores, or to try out their latest flash of inspiration or new phrasing on someone else. Had a door been left ajar? Could you hear snatches of what sounded like Schoenberg's Fourth? It was way past midnight. With outstretched fingers, you pushed against the heavy door, went inside, found the viola player sitting on the edge of the bed, and followed the wildly capricious line of the agitato in the last movement, which, ever since its composition in 1936, gains a bit more truth and clarity with every performance.

Because I was working on a paper about one of the greatest ensembles in the history of string quartets, the Kolisch Quartet of Vienna, I had been given permission to sit in on the lessons given by its former viola player, Eugene Lehner.

A frail old man in a white shirt and gray suit. A teacher, sitting off to one side of the classroom and following the four musicians as they played a composition he knew inside out: Janáček's String Quartet no. 1. This particular piece of music tells a story. Suzanna Flier, the first violinist, is supposed to portray the woman in that story. However, she's focusing on the notes and not thinking about the plot, of which she has only the vaguest idea in any case. The four musicians are seated with their backs to a window overlooking a garden. They and their instructor are connected to each other by a fiery red carpet stretching from one wall to another.

"May I make a remark?"

When I came into the room that morning, the quartet was already playing, and Eugene Lehner had just asked Suzanna Flier for permission to tell her something. May I make a remark? His English was the English of a Central European who remains a Central European even though he's spent half his life in Boston.

He removed his glasses. The quartet waited. There was something slightly apologetic in the gesture he then used to point to a bar in Suzanna Flier's part: This is a mere detail. She followed the aged hand.

"*Tee*-di-dum . . . ," Eugene Lehner sang, bowing in the air with his right arm.

She nodded earnestly.

"A bit longer," he suggested. "I would do it like this." And he pointed, sang, and gestured: "*Ta*-dum, *ta*-dum."

She nodded again, took a pencil, and made a note in her part.

That was it. One of those moments of revelation that would extend far beyond the classroom hours. And when Suzanna Flier started to play again, I could see that she dutifully stayed in contact with her teacher and listened intently to the music. From time to time he leaned in her direction, which she noticed. When she managed to play that particular passage correctly for the second time, he brought his fingers to his lips. "Heaven!" And it was clear to me that she knew, without looking, that his entire face was beaming.

How could she be interested, at this very moment, in the blind music critic? She was chatting away, sipping a glass of Mähler-Bresse kir that he had ordered for her, with her feet up on the chair rung so that her legs were hidden beneath her skirt. In reality, though, she was still in the classroom by the big picture window, where the light spilled across the carpet like red ink.

"That was very feminine, very elegant," Eugene Lehner had said. "The way you played it this time was *so* much more beautiful."

The quartet players were putting away their instruments. It was nearly lunchtime. Suzanna Flier, bent over her violin case, glanced up at the maestro with a look of longing on her face: Really?

"Really," he said. And because he could sense that she wanted to hear more, he added, "The bow change in the legato works quite well."

A moment later the viola player came over and sat down beside him to ask one last question. They were joined by the others. Eugene Lehner nodded and pondered the question, all the while leafing through the score, still in his lap, with an absentminded look on his face.

At last, addressing no one in particular, he made the remark, the suggestion, whose prophetic power — both beautiful and awesome — he could never have suspected in a million years. Those who talk about music do so in a roundabout way.

"Don't *play* the notes," he said kindly, "just humanize them."

We greeted this in silence and thought we understood what he meant.

♪

A little over an hour was left before a bus would take us to the Grand Théâtre in Bordeaux, where the first of the two closing concerts were to be held. Tonight one American and two Hungarian ensembles were scheduled to play; the Schulhoff Quartet was on tomorrow's program. A light buffet was being set up for us in the dining room of the château, since there was to be a formal dinner afterward. I decided to join van Vlooten and Suzanna Flier again. What on earth were the two of them talking about? Unlike most of us, they were oblivious to the strange clouds gathering above Saint-Croix-du-Mont. The hills seemed to recede, and there was talk of one of those sudden storms so typical of this region.

"So, how's it going?"

They both looked up, if you can call van Vlooten's grin a look.

"Fine," said Suzanna Flier. She smiled at me, but didn't let my presence disrupt the conversation she was having with van Vlooten.

"That's true," she admitted. "When you're playing, you're usually wrapped up in your own part."

He: "Aren't you both a player *and* a listener?"

She: "Yes, but you hear the music out of balance."

He: "Even more so, perhaps, because your voice, as first violin, is higher than the rest?"

I noticed that her eyes were now fixed calmly on his face, that they no longer drifted toward the terrace. She replied that the human ear did indeed tend to pick up the higher tones, but that in a quartet it was often the viola, with its seeming modesty, its tendency to melt into the music, that spiced things up.

"A wonderful role," he said when she fell silent. It was clear to me that he was simply priming her voice, hoping to keep her talking. As long as she talked, he could visualize her skin and face, could flesh them out along with her thoughts.

He asked her about the joy of playing in an ensemble.

Her answer was about the pitfalls.

"Sometimes," she began. I knew she was no longer in the classroom, but one door down the hall, on the stage. "Sometimes it all goes well. Everything you've done, the entire process — the training, the rehearsals, the searching, the thinking — it all comes together in . . . now. Your fear falls away. You're filled with excitement."

She knitted her brow. Her nostrils flared.

"Yes?" he said.

"Then you get so carried away by what you're doing that you know it's time to be very, very careful."

She turned her head in my direction and gave

me an inscrutable look. After a few moments of silence, she said, "Well, I'm going upstairs to change. I'll be back in ten minutes."

And she strode off: Suzanna Flier, after a conversation with an intriguing blind man. I'm positive that she enjoyed his attentions and was fascinated by his tragic handicap, but that she wasn't trying to interest the renowned critic — who was here to write a review — in the performance of the Schulhoff Quartet. She wasn't the type to do that. Anyway, as it turned out, the evening wouldn't go as planned. He would not write the review. Marius van Vlooten would fail to send his promised article on the International String Quartet Week at Bordeaux to the *NRC Handelsblad,* or to explain why. That evening he would listen with professional interest to the first of the two concerts. Ignoring the festive reception afterward, he would have himself driven straight back to his hotel, as he usually did. After dictating his initial conclusions into a recorder, he would order a steak bordelaise from room service, drink half a bottle of Château La Rose, and go to bed. In the grip of a very strange mood, he would hear a short storm breaking and in his mind's eye see it sweeping across the entire region, from Montaigne's old tower in the Périgord to Bordeaux's sprawling port, where the Gironde flows in a broad, incredibly wide stream into the Atlantic Ocean.

He leaned closer to me.

"Would you mind telling me something?" he asked, curious. "Was she actually looking at me, or was she glancing around the room as she was talking, or was she looking at you while she was having a conversation with me?"

At me . . . I picked up Suzanna Flier's nearly full glass, which she had left on the table in front of us. So, I thought, not being able to see goes hand in hand with the fear or the suspicion of not being seen. For a moment I closed my eyes and tried to imagine what it must be like to talk to someone who's thinking: What does it matter whether I smile at him, what's the point of reacting, why don't I save my facial expressions for the third person in the company, since my words will reach their target anyway? I drank the sweet-tasting liquid in one gulp. The alcohol went straight to my head.

"She looked into your face with such intensity," I said, "that it seemed as if she was trying to read your thoughts."

♪

She came in through the glass door. She waved at us, but continued on into the dining room. I remember feeling obliged, from a sense of duty born that drunken afternoon, to register her tight dress and high-heeled shoes and to share my observation with my companion,

along with the comment that, like every woman har-
boring a secret love, she was extremely beautiful: viva-
cious, impulsive, tormented, reserved, quiet, apathetic,
demanding, petulant, frenetic, extravagant, indefati-
gable, carefree, impetuous, passionate, as exuberant as
a melody on the G string, as panicky as a tremolo — in
short, as beautiful as the music she had been carrying
around in her head for days.

e had argued about it on the flight from Brussels to Bordeaux.

"Oh, come off it."

"It's true," I insisted. "It does matter."

"No, it doesn't!"

He took a deep breath, shook his head. Even I don't understand why I clung to a theory I hardly believed in. Or at least, not then.

"It does matter," I stubbornly repeated.

Twisting around in the narrow airplane seat to face him, I reduced my analysis of the string quartet to a few short phrases: the love of a woman, the jealousy of her husband, the compassion of the composer. I ticked off all three points on my fingers.

He emitted a low, scornful laugh. "Well, well, well. And you can see all of that in the score?"

"It's, eh . . . ," I began, searching for a concise term that would do justice to the infinitely enigmatic process of composition. "It's *hineingeheimnist,*" I finally said, delighted that one German word could be used to convey the idea that all of that had somehow been mysteriously incorporated into the music.

This time he roared with laughter. He stretched his legs in the aisle and spread his hands wide apart. *"Hineingeheimnist!"* he repeated gleefully.

"Fine," I said after a few moments of huffy silence. "If you would just read Janáček's letter to his adored Kamila, in which he says that while he was composing this work he was thinking of that poor, beaten, tormented woman in Tolstoy's novella."

"Yes, yes," said van Vlooten. "'Music instantly throws me into the spiritual mood in which the composer found himself.'"

In my enthusiasm, I didn't notice his mounting anger. Adopting his lofty tone, I added, "'My soul merges with his and I am taken with him from one mood to another . . .'" He wasn't the only one who could quote Russian classics.

"Hmm," van Vlooten said. "I like my dinners to be followed by something sweet."

"Yes, I do too." I already had the purser in my sights, so I beckoned him over.

He brought us each a profiterole.

"That was the right decision," van Vlooten said with obvious relish, then resumed. "The compassion of the composer! With all due respect, young man, that's nothing more than his own personal warm-up. Since you're so smart, you ought to know that."

"I ought to know that?"

"Yes, you should!"

There was an edge to his voice. It was this edge that made me inquire affably, "So what comes after the warm-up? After what we will assume to be, for the sake of argument, his own genuine excitement?"

"The work, young man. The realm in which music is music."

I licked my fingers. Van Vlooten was busy pulling out a handkerchief. While I unfolded a paper napkin, I began talking about the powerful effects of music on our emotions, something the ancient Greeks knew long ago.

"They considered the Phrygian mode to be sub-versive," I said.

He irritably corrected me.

"You mean the Mixolydian, but I get your point."

"Music manipulates the emotions," I said.

"True. It does indeed."

"But of course it can only trigger an emotion we already have, no matter how latent it is."

He put away his handkerchief, inadvertently jab-bing me with his elbow.

I went on. "Whether you like it or not, this quartet

indisputably deals with a sentiment that is inherently much more powerful than compassion."

He said nothing, but turned his head away, as if he wanted to keep the conversation from continuing.

Softly, just enough to be heard above the drone of the plane, I uttered one small word: "Jealousy."

To distance myself from our dialogue, I began to ponder the viola's tormented screech. The piece had been composed quickly, I thought, in a mere eight days. But he, Janáček, had been walking around with that story in his head for years. When the time is right, such themes apparently present themselves again.

"What are you insinuating?" van Vlooten asked me after about ten minutes had gone by. He had suddenly sat bolt upright in his seat. "Tell me!"

"Nothing at all. I don't know what you're talking about."

Did he get aggressive when he was drunk? I heard him mumbling but couldn't make out the words. Then all of a sudden he shouted, "Kindly remember what I told you about the women in my life!"

I grabbed my cigarettes. "Let's not kick up a fuss," I said, striking a match.

Thinking back to it now, I no longer remember clearly how we found ourselves in the next situation. Beside us, a flight attendant was crouching in the aisle, a dustpan in her hands, sweeping up our broken glasses, while I bent over as far as the cramped space between the seats would allow and tried to pick up the cigarettes that had fallen on the floor, which wasn't easy because the blind man seemed to be doing his best to crush them with his feet.

I left Château Mähler-Bresse on the fifteenth
of August, two days after the master class had
ended and the last concert had been played. The
flight to Amsterdam left at 7:00 P.M. after a delay of
about twenty minutes. The boarding had been rather
hurried, so it wasn't until after takeoff that a very
young flight attendant took her place in the aisle to
explain the safety procedures. I shifted my gaze from
the landscape to the girl, who was demonstrating, with
an earnest expression on her face, how to fasten a ficti-
tious seat belt around her waist. Staring straight ahead,
she said, "Pull the strap tighter," then proceeded to
do so. Next she said, "Lock your tray into the seat in
front of you and return your seat to the upright position." There was a faint tremor of anxiety in her voice,
and I suspected that this was one of the first times
she had been allowed to address the passengers on
board. Yet all I could think of was that this silvery tube,

packed with human lives, was now climbing its way diagonally into the sky. Flying is the safest way to travel, I told myself, with the memory of last week's crash at Heathrow still fresh in my mind. The statistics bear this out with the numerical consistency of a law of nature. While the flight attendant was asking us to extinguish our cigarettes, I wondered if there was such a thing as a law of danger, which hadn't been discovered yet, but which threatened us one individual at a time, with a decided preference for bizarre details. Earlier this afternoon Suzanna Flier had attempted to free a black butterfly that had flown into her room. She had climbed up on the windowsill and, falling out of her third-floor window, she let out a loud scream and immediately grabbed one of the sturdier shoots of the Gloire de Bordeaux, the wild grape that flourishes on southwesterly walls in this region.

Marius van Vlooten had been in the room with her. Only after the initial panic had died down, only after she had taken a few sips of wine to calm herself as she sat on the stone steps to the terrace, did Suzanna Flier remember him. Her eyes roamed over the friends who had rushed to her aid, lighted on mine, and beckoned me. "Marius . . . ," she said, one hand clutching to her bosom the stiff, snowy white tablecloth that a waiter had snatched off a table — she had been nude. Suzanna Flier cast a meaningful glance at the window of what I knew to be her bedroom.

I found him in a sorry state in the hallway on the third floor. In those days Marius van Vlooten was a physically fit, well-mannered man who managed, in spite of his blindness, to dress with a certain flair. I now found him about ten feet away from the stairs in a wrinkled pair of ash-colored trousers and a crookedly buttoned shirt with the tails flapping. As I watched, he groped the air, turning this way and that to find the wall, brushing instead against an arrangement of peacock feathers in a tall vase on a low taboret. He jerked his hands away, as if in fright, and it was then that I noticed the look of terror on his face, the look of alarm that I immediately realized couldn't possibly be for himself and had nothing to do with reality, with the facts. For surely he had heard his girlfriend being rescued.

"Everything's okay," I said after I led him back to her room and we were sitting side by side on the edge of the bed. I began by recounting the part he had undoubtedly been able to follow with his own ears through the open window: that a couple of young musicians had been sitting around talking in the shade of the orangerie, even though it was siesta time; that in the background, from the direction of the greenhouse, there had been the occasional scrape of a shovel as the gardener mixed sand and lime. All of this had been drowned out by the shrill cry of "Help!" followed by three or four minutes in which Suzanna Flier had clung to the vines, while below her a ladder had been shoved against the wall and quickly extended to the third floor. She had descended like a goddess, landed in a bed of lavender, which must have felt warm beneath her feet, and moaned, "Gosh, that scared the living daylights out of me."

He didn't seem at all interested. He said nothing, just breathed heavily. We sat for a bit on the rumpled bed while I stared at the panties, the white cane, and the yellow dress scattered across the floor and felt beside me, almost palpably, the dreadful panic, the fear that a loved one will die, though in the interim real life has simply, and with an utter lack of drama, moved on.

His jaw was still tightly clenched. At last he spoke. "I have to throw up, or I'll choke."

I helped him to the bathroom, lifted the toilet seat, and made sure he was crouched at the right angle.

♪

First she stretched her right arm endearingly toward one side of the cabin, then her left arm: the emergency exits. She explained that if the lights went out, there would be emergency lighting in the aisles. I leaned toward the window to take one last look at the Gironde estuary — an immense, magnificent view. Does she have any idea, I thought, how much it means to him? Does she realize that it's been twenty years since he was so smitten by a woman? I was convinced, at the time, that Suzanna Flier had begun her affair with the blind man the way a woman usually begins an affair: playful and passionate, a brief whirl to find out if she's desired. Casting in your lot with another person is a different matter altogether.

Little by little, I had heard from various sources how the two of them had reached an understanding. I had frequently been in their company, but had failed to observe their growing intimacy for the simple reason that I hadn't been paying attention. But in hindsight one thing is sure: the twenty minutes in which Marius van Vlooten let the love motif, with its own virtually uncontrollable force, back into his life again are the twenty minutes in which the Schulhoff Quartet played a *Kreutzer* Sonata that made the sparks fly.

"He sat there like a rock," the second violinist of the Anonymous Quartet told me afterward in the foyer. He had sat next to the critic during the concert and had felt such a strong physical reaction when his neighbor, who had been leaning slightly forward in his seat, suddenly stiffened and turned to stone, that he glanced at him several times out of the corner of his eye. Furthermore, he had noted that the blind man's staring face and tightly closed eyes had been focused on the players as if he could actually see all four of them.

"No," I replied. "Not all four of them, just her. Suzanna Flier was the only one he could see."

The fair-haired young man eyed me curiously. We were standing in the middle of the post-concert crowd with our drinks in our hands. I saw him smile and suspected that his inner eye was picturing the first violinist in her green silk concert dress with her hair in an elegant chignon. But I knew all too well which portrait the blind man had been envisioning ever since yesterday: a woman in yellow, a braid hanging down her back, her white arms moving without the slightest reserve, the bow in her right hand racing across the strings and the fingers of her left hand doing their meticulous work, though she tries to keep her face under control.

The four string players were sitting in a formation customary in Haydn's day, as van Vlooten no doubt heard the moment they began to play: the two violins on the outside, the cello and viola on the inside. It lends a certain balance to the sound, which we, the seeing audience, can observe with our eyes and subsequently signal to our ears: Oh, look, the cello is next to the first violin, what a lovely sound. The moment van Vlooten reached the same conclusion, however, his attention had already shifted onto a different plane. Because his world, transparent, infinitely vast, consists entirely of the audible, things that are heard in disconnected fragments, in conjectures that cease abruptly as soon as they stop producing sound: Trees are only trees as long as the wind blows, an entire block of houses on a quiet Monday morning vanishes from the face of the earth until someone flings open a window, landscapes rush by like ghosts on either side of a pounding train. . . . Anyway, the quartet had started to play, and van Vlooten had leaned forward in his seat. Perhaps he had thought only fleetingly, vaguely, of Suzanna Flier that day, but he must have pictured her now, sitting there so clearly in her cotton sundress, because things that make a sound announce their existence, and also tell us how and where. I was sitting much farther away that evening, on the right side of the hall, and I still remember how utterly spellbinding the quartet was. The magic was there from the start, the magic of a continuum that never stops, not even for real life, which seizes every opportunity — coughing, rustling, the shuffling of feet, the tuning of strings — to thrust its way to the fore.

"I was glad they played the four movements with almost no break in between," the Scottish violinist said to me.

I agreed and said that, in my opinion, it had also been Janáček's wish. The violinist nodded. He knew what I meant. "He wanted just a slight pause."

"Yes."

"He wanted a fast-paced story."

We stared at each other.

"Yes," I said. "What he had in mind was a fatal psychological drama that no earthly power could bring to a halt."

Looking away from the Scot, I caught sight of van Vlooten on the other side of the foyer. He was standing by himself in the doorway to the balcony, with his back to the room. His head, sticking out above the crowd, was silhouetted against the night-blue cupola of a building across the street.

♪

I never listen. In a situation of total panic, would you really be able to grab one of those things, those flimsy masks, and fit it neatly over your nose and mouth? The flight attendant standing in front of me had managed most of it. All she had to do was slip the elastic over her hairdo. But the power of suggestion is so great that I reached up and adjusted the air vent above my head until I felt a breeze in my face. *"Wind, why do you still caress this body,"* suddenly flashed into my head, and at the same moment I remembered that there had been a pleasant draft last night in the Grand Théâtre.

It had been more than welcome. The eighteenth-century Grand Théâtre has three tiers of closely packed plush seats. And because the short storm the day before had not brought cool relief but quite the opposite, the air coming in from the corridors was extremely sultry — sultry and oppressive. Which made it all the nicer when the downstairs doors let in that flow of air, that invisible caress that united the audience in the lowest tier, or rather united them even more since they had already felt waves of heat and masses of emotion pass over them collectively. They all heard the first violinist play the C#–D–C#–B–C#–F#–D–C#–B motif, signifying a confirmation and a secret pleasure, and heard the cellist's grave reply. How odd it was, I now mused, for eight hundred people to listen, as one, to a story consisting of eight hundred different versions.

And to watch the quartet. The viola player, sitting at an angle, was a tall, dark musician who followed the bidding of the notes with a furious bowing while the muscles in his face twitched frequently but enigmatically. The second violin pressed his heels firmly to the ground when it was his turn to race along for bars and bars, and there was an angry look in his eyes. Sometimes you only find out afterward what you suspected all along: Marius van Vlooten had not only stared exclusively at the first violinist — how could he have done otherwise? — but had also primarily followed her part.

It was no ordinary evening. Just the day before, Suzanna Flier herself had said to the critic, "When you're playing, you hear the music out of balance." So now, in the story being told in music this evening, she was playing her own melodic line, the fate allotted to her in the story. To a musician, this is never a passive process, because for fate to find you, you must open the gates wide. That's exactly what she did that evening, and van Vlooten heard it and followed her, without realizing, of course, that in the intoxicating glow of her concentration she had been clinging to something, to the instructions, the mysterious clue that her teacher had hesitatingly, after a meditative pause, finally put into words.

Don't play *the notes, just humanize them.*

Who knows what the aging maestro had in mind when he made this comment?

Not the marital tragedy, I'm sure of that, since musicians think in abstract terms. Nor the ill-fated story from which the music sprang, about an oppressive marriage, about a Beethoven sonata, about the death of an attractive, musical woman whose adultery was never actually established but who was nevertheless stabbed to death with a dagger. The listening audience doesn't think of a speeding coach or a pair of galloping horses either, but simply allows the sounds to rain down on them like a fountain of alien emotions on the emotions already in their hearts. It's true. But there were also two music lovers in that concert hall who had gotten into a fight during their flight from Brussels to Bordeaux. Who had, at a late hour in a droning plane, exercised their imaginations and argued about whether it mattered that you could, if you wanted to, locate the exact spot in a score where a man's fury rises to the danger point.

♪

It's not easy for a blind person to meet a certain someone at a busy reception. Especially if that someone, a violinist, has no specific reason to talk to you and is barely aware of your presence.

"He asked me to look around the room for him," the female cellist of the United States' Jefferson Quartet told me the next day. The tall girl, towering over the crowd like van Vlooten, had told the blind man that a lovely buffet had been set up along the entire back wall, to his right; she had described the dishes as well as she could from a distance, and she had offered to help him fill his plate. "But all he wanted to know was who was standing in line, who was milling around, and who was sitting at the tables," she said.

It was the evening after the concert, the final evening of the International String Quartet Week, and everyone was rushing around in a last-minute effort to cement friendships made during the week. Van Vlooten, white cane in hand, stood tall and straight amid the throng as if he were occupying a place of honor, though no one took any particular notice of him. People bumped into him, apologized, offered him a drink, and asked him, obligingly enough, if they could perhaps be of service.

"Yes, indeed. I'd like to speak to someone from the Schulhoff Quartet."

So at some point he suddenly found himself face to face with the quartet's viola player, who politely leaned closer to hear what the critic wished to ask him. Nothing. Van Vlooten emptied his glass; another was pressed into his hand. He was introduced to two men. It was all quite casual. He didn't catch their names. They exchanged a few polite remarks about the sultry air still drifting in from outside and paused for a moment to listen to a distant clap of thunder, after which van Vlooten repeated his wish: to speak to someone from the Schulhoff Quartet. By that time the party was in full swing, with everyone in the grip of the enchantment that descends on a gathering of young, beautiful, somewhat neurotic talents, who flutter around each other like a flock of birds before heading off, one by one or in groups, to their further destinations.

I don't know why van Vlooten didn't simply ask for Suzanna Flier or ask someone to take him to her. When I ran into him, he had been waylaid by a short, perspiring woman who was chatting away, but she was so small and it was so noisy that he probably didn't even hear the tiny voice down by his stomach. I had just made the round of the buffet tables and was passing by with a heaping plate in my hand when I caught sight of him.

"Mr. van Vlooten!"

He immediately turned in my direction. His face was covered with red blotches. Holding my plate in one hand and cupping his elbow with the other, I led him toward the dining area, and as he tapped his way across the parquet — one tap for each step — I listed all the appetizers I had piled on my plate for him and promised to go back soon for seconds. As if by secret arrangement, I didn't take my friend directly to his lady friend either. Or rather, I did, but I worded it differently. "Look," I said, "there's Eugene Lehner. Shall I introduce you to him?"

The Hungarian maestro was seated at the corner of several tables that had been pushed together by his master-class students. To his left, at the head of the table, was Suzanna Flier, clutching her knife and fork and leaning over to ask him a question or make a remark. When Marius van Vlooten sat down on the other side of her, on a chair I had fetched for him, she glanced over her shoulder and flashed him a quick, useless smile, but stayed as she was, with her back to him. Van Vlooten took a few tentative bites, and I perched beside him, snatching an occasional tidbit from his plate without his being aware of it, while Lehner, urged on by everyone at the table, resumed the anecdote that he had been telling. And that I remember, after many years, as follows.

It was late in the summer of 1927. Lehner and

the other three members of the Kolisch Quartet were staying in the Hotel Americain in Amsterdam. Twice that week they were scheduled to play a combined Schoenberg and Beethoven program in the Concert-gebouw. On one of their nights off, the four musicians were heading up to their rooms after dining in the hotel restaurant when they suddenly came to a halt on the stairs to the second floor. Each of them had the feeling, independently of the others, that he must be hallucinating, for the faint but unmistakable sound of two violins, a viola, and a cello could be heard coming from the direction of their rooms. Holding their breaths, they tiptoed farther, instinctively trying to place the unknown but vaguely familiar music. They finally reached their two adjoining rooms. As in a dream, they threw open the doors. To their surprise, there wasn't a soul in sight. Their eyes flew to the windows, which had been left open because of the sweltering weather. The music, clearly swelling now, was definitely coming from outside. And from above their heads. "Bartók," suggested one of the musicians, while another pointed his finger in the air and said, "Kodály, with a slight touch of Martinů."

Meanwhile their surprise had been replaced by something else. How should they approach the mystery or respond to it? What should their answer to its summons be? Within minutes, Kolisch and Kuhner, the violinists, Lehner, the viola player, and Heifetz, the cellist, had taken their instruments from their cases, gone out into the hallway, climbed the stairway to the third floor, peeked through the door of Room 309, and discovered the source of their wild imaginings: the four members of the Bohemian Quartet, who also happened to be in Amsterdam, playing Janáček. Remember, it was a hot and sultry evening. Windows had been flung open all over the city. The sounds of the *Kreutzer* Sonata, whose published score had not yet seen the light of day, poured out over Leidseplein and rose up the fabled gables. The two string quartets, blissfully happy, played to each other half the night. Hotel guests hung out the windows, and from the street came a burst of applause.

♪

The thunderstorm broke shortly before dawn. I was sound asleep with my head under the covers when I was jolted awake by the words in my dream: "*In general, music is a dreadful thing. Why is that?*" For a moment I felt confused and didn't know where I was. Then I saw the windowsill and the flash of lightning beyond it.

The château's annex had been placed at right angles to the main building. Throwing a sweater around my shoulders, I walked over to the window to watch the storm and couldn't help seeing the bedrooms of my friends and acquaintances, some of them empty tonight, others doubly occupied, as they lit up and faded into darkness again. Then, over in the corner where the two wings came together, I caught sight of someone standing, like me, by the window, a motionless shadow, too far away to make out the features. But I imagined that he, van Vlooten, felt himself being enveloped in a canopy of thunder and pictured him breathing in the distant aroma of lightning. He too must have heard the rain drumming on the roof of the Renault Estafette, the hotel van parked in the drive, which at the beginning of the evening had taken several members of our group to Bordeaux and much later brought them back again through the pitch-dark blackness of the night.

A morous urges are triggered by circumstances, I thought, finally stretching my
legs. The young woman had finally finished her spiel,
having turned it into quite a production. After the
oxygen mask, she had explained the lifejacket, showing us how to pull the tab and blow into the tube, and
even getting us to bend over and feel under our seats,
and sure enough, there was the lifejacket, a real credit
to her teaching methods, and then she had announced
the airline's special duty-free offers, this time with
the PA system turned up to full blast.

The class was now being rewarded with a treat,
nuts and sodas, and allowed to press the seatback buttons and stare contentedly at the clear blue sky. As
for me, I began thinking almost immediately of the
biology class I had taken in my sophomore year of
high school, in which it was explained that erotic
impulses in animals are not merely a reaction to the

state of their hormones. The female porcupine prefers to seduce the male of her choice early in the morning, with her quills relaxed so that they're lying flat on the damp ground; the Taiwanese rat snake likes to mate in the spring just after he emerges, half dazed, from hibernation and his reproductive organs haven't quite reached their full potential; the male hawfinch spurns his partner, for no apparent physical reason, when it's not windy or rainy; stormy weather acts as a stimulus, and then it takes him only a few minutes to get the job done. So it's not inconceivable that we humans also need certain conditions to put us in the right mood.

The morning of August 14 began pure and cool. It was the kind of morning in which you feel happy without wondering why. Suzanna Flier must have come downstairs around nine o'clock. Since she and the other members of the Schulhoff Quartet had said good-bye to their teacher the night before — Lehner's flight left at 8:10 A.M. — I imagine that she began her day by casting a cheerful glance around the dining room, and lo and behold, there was van Vlooten next to the swinging doors, bent over, feeling the floor with his fingertips. She saw a room key, attached to a big copper ball, near his right foot.

"There," she said with a nod, after going over and saying hello. "Just behind your right foot. Yes, there."

They went out to sit at one of the tables on the

terrace, still wet from last night's storm, and ordered a huge English breakfast.

"They looked like a pair of wolves," I was told by a Flemish journalist who had ridden down in the elevator with Suzanna Flier. From where she had been sitting at a nearby table, she got the impression that the two of them were on intimate terms. They ate from each other's plates. They did things with their hands. She plucked a nasturtium from one of the pots on the terrace, and he snatched it from her, filled it with honey, held the edible flower up to where he assumed her mouth was, and knocked over the coffeepot, which they had already drunk to the last drop anyway.

"I'm an incredibly clumsy man," he said.

Then they talked about what they were going to do that day. He suggested the zoo. She thought about it, moving her head from side to side as she weighed the options. "You know," he said, "I'm crazy about animals," and he began telling her about a monkey that friends of his parents used to have years ago, a little monster with cheek pouches on either side of his head, which, when stuffed with goodies, bore a great resemblance, in terms of size as well as logic, to the bulging pair of pink anal appurtenances down below. "I liked to pet him, though he would suddenly frown, press his lips together, prick up his ears, grab your clothes with all four hands, and let out a shriek."

She calmly replied, "I was planning to go to an exhibition at the Musée Biraud. Apparently they've brought together a number of very nice Picassos."

"He stared at her for a moment, absolutely speechless," the Flemish journalist told me. "But then he seemed to think it was an excellent idea."

An excellent idea, yes, it certainly must have been. In fact, it must have been a five-star outing, to judge by what a handful of us who were staying on in the château — which hospitable Bordeaux had continued to put at our disposal — were able to report later that afternoon. "He was on cloud nine when they came in," said one. "Yes," remarked another, "he said he'd seen a favorite painting of his, a portrait that he remembered from ages ago in Berlin."

♪

The hotel van had driven them and several other guests into Bordeaux. They had asked to be dropped off at the rue Bonnier so they could stroll along the esplanade Charles de Gaulle in the direction of what used to be the center of town. The sun was already hot. Standing on the gravel beneath an enormous mulberry tree was a juggler, a young man in baggy black pants who managed to keep eight pins moving in geometrical patterns above his head without dropping a single one. "I love things like that," Suzanna Flier later told a friend. So she paused for a moment, without a word of explanation to her companion, though she did have her hand on his forearm, because that's how they had been walking. As she watched, he listened to the comments of the spectators, and after they walked on, the whole thing came together: the young man who managed to keep eight pins moving in geometrical patterns above his head without dropping a single one was a college dropout, a quiet genius who had stopped going to classes from one day to the next and to his dying day would be a potentially brilliant theoretical physicist.

"The poor boy was so pale," Suzanna Flier said. "Jugglers are fearful types," she added. "Apparently, they're more fearful than any other circus artists, even more fearful than trapeze artists. Does that make sense?"

"I think so."

Meanwhile they were going up the steps to the museum. Suzanna Flier was eager to see the paintings, so she didn't worry about whether van Vlooten could negotiate the hard slabs of glinting marble, though in fact he did just fine. Blind people feel comfortable and secure on a series of evenly spaced steps with a railing up the side.

Musée Biraud was a little-known museum on a side street in an old neighborhood. The square-shaped building consisted of a series of interconnected rooms that could be reached by a set of semicircular stairs. In the middle of the atrium on the ground floor was a palm tree that had grown all the way up to the second floor, where there was a bubbling fountain, which seemed, thanks to the building's deceptive acoustics, to follow them everywhere.

They had been handed a ticket and a floor plan.

Suzanna Flier briefly studied the sheet of paper, then suggested that they start downstairs in the leftmost gallery, which housed the French Baroque painters. He agreed. She took his hand and placed it on her arm. Almost immediately she fell into a strange, disoriented mood, brought on by the oasis-like burbling of the fountain and the silent white rooms of unknown objects awaiting her. "Oddly enough," she later said, "I was glad he had his cane with him. That tap-tap-tap on the parquet floor was actually quite pleasant."

There were hardly any other visitors, which surprised her, since it was such an extraordinarily beautiful museum. The first gallery they entered was deserted, except for a man in a cobalt blue suit disappearing around the corner on the far side of the room. She started describing the first painting she happened to see — a Poussin. By a mere stiffening of her body, she had signaled to van Vlooten that he should come to a standstill, not too close to the canvas and yet not too far away, and then she had told him what he was looking at: a landscape. After the first trees and temples, she got a bit flustered when he mentioned the oxcart, not quite in the middle of the composition, then drew her attention to the two men in the foreground carrying the bier of their dead friend from the left side of the canvas to the right. He was familiar with the painting. She looked at his face, very close to hers, and listened vaguely as he mumbled something about the colors, which he compared to the later Titian, and bit her lips, puzzled by her own confusion.

Another room, the same milky white light, the gurgle of the fountain. The water appeared to be getting heavier, she thought; it was now splashing down even more emphatically. Still, he didn't seem to notice, or at any rate gave no indication that he had. He simply repeated cheerfully and with a great deal of interest the titles of the paintings she pointed out to him, or else screwed his face into a frown and said nothing. Claude Lorrain. La Tour. "La Tour!" he echoed, and immediately asked which work. Having observed that there wasn't a guard in sight, she led him close to the painting. And while he breathed in the spectacular light and shadows, then shook his head, pressed her arm, and walked on, she wondered if she might have a fever. Where am I, she thought two staircases, two rooms, and a short hallway later, and what on earth am I doing? Actually, she had just left Watteau and moved on rather incongruously to a small row of

seventeenth-century Dutch painters that at first —
carried along by the momentum of her own voice,
which kept bubbling on and on like the water — she
hadn't even been able to identify. She saw the man in
the cobalt blue suit, the typical garb of French sculptors
and painters, approach from the opposite direction
and look at them in passing as if to say: I understand.
His silent salute, aimed at her but meant for both of
them, went unanswered. "Oh, look," she said a few
seconds later, and for the first time gave the painting
the kind of attention that artistic miracles demand of
you. She saw a woman in a dimly lit interior, sitting
by a window and reading a letter. Yes, she thought
approvingly, sitting idly on your backside, so calm in
your place in the world — you are your body — and
at the same moment she became aware of a small
practical problem that had been bothering her all
along: how should she offer her lips to a man who
couldn't see them, who was only interested in paintings, and whose blind blue eyes positively glowed;
how could she use her words to express an emotion
that couldn't even be expressed in words? "A woman in
her living room," she reported, which gave her some
measure of relief. "A wide-open window. A wide-
open door. A dog..." She took her arm out from
under his, feeling gratifyingly down-to-earth, though
her fingers tingled, as they often do after a shock.

"What do you think," he calmly suggested, "time for the Picassos?"

She agreed that it was a good idea. What they found, after wandering in and out of various rooms, were women — standing in front of mirrors, sitting on red chairs, sitting on blue chairs, reclining, lying on yellow divans, lying in a man's embrace — the female nudes painted by Picasso in the 1930s, during a period of exceptionally sex-driven inspiration. She described the paintings to him. She spoke with cool precision, but she also looked at them with the greatest of personal interest. Images go much faster than words, as she soon found out. The figures immediately dredged up memories, searing and intense. These women were obliging, uncomplicated, and acquiescent, even in repose, for it was not just male pleasure that was being depicted here. Meanwhile she described their colors and shapes as accurately as she could, and this cool description for his benefit gave her a feeling of satisfaction not unlike that of certain intimate phone conversations, which also falter now and then. How is that kiss of ours ever going to happen? she wondered. And she began to long for a dimly lit cab that would carry them back to Château Mähler-Bresse at a calm, unhurried pace.

"Where's the portrait of Dora Maar?" his voice boomed, just one step away from her.

They must have stood in front of the picture for ten minutes, she guessed afterward, if not longer. He knew it from years ago in Berlin, he told her, a painting of a woman in a yellow sweater, with a snazzy bluish violet hat on her head. What luck to find it here, on temporary loan, right before his very nose, and he started to elaborate on the wonderful immobility of the model, who sat there like a queen, a Persephone, with her hands on the arms of her chair, looking at you with one of her eyes staring straight ahead and the other off to the side.

This time she was the listener, or rather she heard him talking but was completely deaf to the "alabaster-white face" of the girl and her "clamplike hands." She'd had enough new impressions, she felt. Not to mention that she was fed up with the splashing of the fountain, now drowning out everything else and somehow transformed into a new and more persistent form of anxiety about their kiss. She leaned forward. "Shall we go?" she said close to his ear and was somewhat surprised when his hand immediately sought her arm. Yes, of course. Once again she studied the floor plan. She didn't want either of them to have to take one step more than absolutely necessary in this maze, but luckily they didn't have to, for there was the exit and the bright white steps, and she was momentarily dazzled by the sudden sun and daylight, but then she managed to flag down a cab with a wild wave of her arm and dive into its comfy lair after him. They had already driven off when she thought she heard the pounding of rain on the roof.

♪

I was waiting in the entryway for my cab and saw them come into the lobby. His hand on her elbow, his face dark, he still didn't seem his usual self. I hesitated. Should I go over and say good-bye again? They walked toward the lounge, which also led into the garden. Suzanna Flier had on her yellow dress, which she must have hung up after scooping it up off the floor, for it fell in smooth folds around her body. You could tell that she had already forgotten her potentially deadly fall and was concentrating on just one thing: What shall we do next? Until then she had probably not been bored. They had apparently gone to the zoo that morning, one with a wildlife preserve in which the predatory animals perched in the trees like cats. An olfactory paradise of piss, dung, and musk, or so I imagined it, whose roaring, sniffing, braying, screeching, and quacking must have been graphic enough, even for someone whose eyes are permanently shut. God knows what's going on between the two of them, I thought, and glanced at my watch. A moment later Suzanna Flier looked at hers.

That was the last time I saw her. Behind me a horn honked. I picked up my bag and let myself be driven to the airport.

9

en years after I had flown to Bordeaux with Marius van Vlooten, I came back to Europe for a short stay and ran into the music critic at one of the check-in counters at Schiphol Airport. Because my work had obliged me to move to Princeton immediately after our first meeting, the summery week at the château had quickly been forgotten. But even fate seems to work on a smaller scale on this continent, placing me ten years later in line behind van Vlooten. We struck up a conversation, and I noticed that he was in a disagreeable mood.

The girl behind the counter didn't do much to improve it.

"A window seat or an aisle seat?" she asked, her eyes glued to the monitor.

Van Vlooten emitted a short laugh. I moved up to stand beside him. "He prefers to sit on the aisle," I said to the girl, and plunked down my ticket and passport. "You can give me the window seat."

Scowling, he walked beside me toward the passport-control gate. I could see that he knew the way and said something to that effect. "Until they decide to remodel the place again," he replied. "Until this stupid country gets another urge to expand, pollute, and make a terrific din so that a bunch of idiots can fly to Spain at rock-bottom prices!"

No sooner had we turned a corner on our way to Gate G than we came upon a plywood hoarding, behind which a bunch of pneumatic drills were blasting away, their hellish staccato drowning out a popular radio station with one of those slur-your-words-together male voices that drive you insane. It's a wonder we were able to hear the airport announcement that Flight ZD 421 to Salzburg had been temporarily delayed.

"God almighty!" van Vlooten said a quarter of an hour later, his fingers touching the base of a champagne glass. We had finally found a bar, all gleaming chrome and mirrors, set down like an island in the middle of a suffocatingly busy corridor. The smell of oysters and fish filled the air; the only drink served was champagne. "Ghastly stuff," van Vlooten said to the person he sensed was occupying the bar stool on his right. The anonymous man, likewise stranded, was able to inform him that the forty-eight-year-old pilot of our plane had been grounded. Yes, it was indeed due to alcohol, and well over the 0.2 legal limit.

"A Romanian," van Vlooten reported back to me. "Now sleeping it off for the required four hours." And his voice, suddenly as muffled and toneless as a person immobilized by a fire, caused me to glance sideways. His downcast eyes had dark circles underneath, and his jaw was moving as if he were chewing something.

I asked him how he was doing after all these years.

He said that she had left him two weeks ago.

Not wanting immediately to appear to know who he was referring to, I tactfully inquired, "Your wife?"

"Suzanna."

And he told me that he had received a letter from her lawyer early this morning, just after he had finished shaving and getting dressed. "The mail always arrives at our house before nine."

"Please read it to me," he had said to his servant, the butler-cum-chauffeur whom he treated without reserve for the simple reason that he couldn't afford to do otherwise. At that moment he was sitting in the kitchen, at his usual place, where he normally sat at precisely quarter to eight every morning to eat breakfast with Suzanna and their six-year-old son. It was a gorgeous day. Behind him, the door to the vegetable garden was open, and anyone with a sensitive ear could have deduced from the cackling of the chickens that it was hot and sunny outside. Marius van Vlooten, who hadn't slept for three nights, was not listening, but was holding up a tablespoon of coffee in which he was dissolving a couple of aspirins. "Read it!" he ordered, then brought the spoon to his mouth, swallowed, and began to stir the coffee in his outsize cup, which he found within easy reach at the exact spot where it was supposed to be.

One place setting. Across from him, two empty chairs. His wife was suing for divorce on the grounds of mental cruelty, asking for a steep — though certainly not unreasonable — alimony, and demanding child custody.

I listened in surprise, first of all because the two of them had evidently been together all this time. That he, van Vlooten, had been swept off his feet all those years ago was something I hadn't forgotten, but I thought of Suzanna Flier as a woman who lived only for her art, though of course the light, carefree side of her personality wouldn't say no to an amorous adventure now and then, as you could tell by looking at her. How had he managed to claim her for life? At the same moment I said to myself, as if the words had been whispered in my ear, Ah, nothing makes the fires of love burn brighter than the knowledge that you have something, a power, a unique ability, to inspire another human being with passion.

My glance shifted to the traveling hordes, who kept parting down the middle like a flock of sheep as they skirted around the bar. T-shirts. Blank faces. The same plodding gait. Yet I couldn't help thinking that, given the right stimulus, any one of them could be transformed into a terrifying creature bereft of all reason.

Meanwhile, van Vlooten was muttering something about bloodshed and murder.

I took a sip of the so-called champagne and was about to ask, "What the devil are you talking about?" when he assured me, almost solemnly, that a clever blind person can accomplish any number of things, including murder.

He noted my skepticism. "I heard your snort of contempt!" he exclaimed.

"Well, uh ... ," I began, then bent over to retrieve the white cane I had accidentally knocked to the floor. He took it from me impatiently and leaned it back against the bar. "Never start plotting an act of evil with the idea 'I'll see where this takes me,'" he said vehemently. And after describing a circle in the air with one hand, he added, "Because not all of them can be stopped!"

As if we had asked for another round, the bar-maid slapped two more glasses of champagne down in front of us. We drank. In the tone of voice used for pleasant, lighthearted conversation, I asked him what kind of thing a clever blind person can accomplish "in daily life."

He replied without a moment of hesitation. "Skiing."

"Really?"

Yes.

They always went to Morgélès to ski, staying in the hotel he used to stay in with his parents and his sister Emily. Later, when a chauffeur had been added to their household, Suzanna enjoyed climbing into the back seat to sit beside her husband, but in the first few years she had been the one to drive the car. Sometimes she even drove all the way from their house in Wassenaar to the foot of the Vosges Mountains — a six-hour drive — without having to brake once. That shows how skillfully she operated the vehicle and how well she understood his dark, boundless world. As she drove she would mutter to herself the names on the signboards, along with the number of miles to the next place, a habit that suited him, since it gave him the opportunity to draw an exact map of the area in his head. She always stopped, without fail, at the Routiers in Saint-Dié, and after the first time she no longer needed to say, "Stairs ten steps ahead of you. Turn left after fifty yards," because he could easily find his way to the restaurant, where he would stride over to an empty table, one step behind her. Then, and this was the part he really liked, she would casually place his hand on the back of a chair so he would know where to sit.

Small things? Which you often remember more clearly than the big fateful ones?

Nothing, absolutely nothing, about her was small. The tinkle of her bracelet? The beckoning of fate. Or when she leaned swiftly forward in the Routiers to say, "Your napkin's fallen in your glass"? The whispering of a demon. Being in love with your own wife is an appalling business, which transforms the entire world into a cavernous abyss of restlessness and dreams. Yes, it does, and by the time the next morning had come to an end, he had hurled himself with total confidence down the swooshing mountainside.

Heavens no, it wasn't at all difficult. In the first place, he had skied as a child, so he was able to hire an experienced instructor from the village who made him practice on the kiddie slope for an hour before accompanying him on the run, shouting instructions at him in the gritty cold, which he could feel rushing beneath him like a razor-edged mirage, down into the depths below, until he reached the place at the end where it started going up again, which he could predict with perfect precision. It was a piece of cake. The other reason it wasn't difficult was that she, Suzanna, would be waiting for him at the bottom of the slope, cheerful and interested, though she herself had never gone skiing and wasn't about to because of her violin

("Aha! So she's still playing?"—"Well, for goodness sake, why wouldn't she be!"), anyway there she stood, ready to embrace him in her downy quilt jacket with the elasticized sleeves, which allowed him to thrust his hands inside and grab her by the elbows.

*O*h, come on! You didn't think we would? Why not? Can you think of one good reason why she and I should *not* have gone on seeing each other? Oh. I can't imagine what you mean by that."

Several times I noticed that he kept his eyes on mine while he was talking, as though he could actually see me. And now he was even wagging his finger in my direction. The fixed stare that I remembered from our previous encounter had disappeared. She had probably said to him, "Look at where my voice is coming from." Meanwhile the clock across from us was pointing to six-thirty. That part of the population that was on the move was still pressing in on us. Most of the passengers looked as if they had been sentenced to hard labor. Van Vlooten told me that he and Suzanna Flier had moved into a house with a gatekeeper's cottage, in the dunes by Wassenaar, where you could smell the sea breeze, though not the sea itself.

"Everything in the house will be exactly as you want it to be, Suzanna," he had told her, "but the furniture can't be moved so much as an inch."

The last part may have sounded a bit drastic, but she didn't mind. Together with him, she cheerfully put heart and soul into creating a house in which everything occupied its own space according to certain geometrical principles. What makes houses so complicated is not the floor plan, which is usually a clear drawing, but the interior decoration. This house had been designed in the shape of a rectangle, with an entryway on the first floor, a kitchen fifteen steps away, a living room centered around a huge fireplace, and, through another door, a side room five steps long and six steps wide, which was perfect for his study. The bedrooms and a couple of charming little rooms they didn't have use for just yet were on the second floor. The attic on the top floor, her practice room, had been remodeled. Skylights had been added, along with a narrow wooden balcony, where he would occasionally find her in a mood he couldn't quite define.

The real game therefore began when the furniture arrived. "Here, please," he said to the movers, tapping his foot on the parquet, and a cabinet was lowered into place. And so it went with the rest of their belongings. The movers, no doubt put at ease by Suzanna's laughing assurance that she agreed with it all, had traipsed along behind him with the whole kit and caboodle, including the coatrack, the doormats, and the stereo, while he briskly led the way and sometimes, stubbornly insistent, made them shift a piece of furniture an inch or two. That evening, and on the days that followed, he and Suzanna applied themselves to the awesome task of arranging the drawers and cupboards.

"Stop being so finicky!" she said at the end of the week, in a state of total exhaustion. By then the entire house had been made cozy and warm and everything was all but nailed into place. He had reproached her for putting the ashtray to the left rather than to the right of the stack of mail on the table. She has a point, he thought, sliding his fingertips over the smooth, polished tabletop. I know I'm an absolute pain in the neck. Yet he wasn't ashamed of himself. A few days later he snapped at her, "Who moved the chair so close to the middle?"

"What?" For a moment she was too flabbergasted to say anything. Then she told him that a delivery man had dropped by that afternoon, and she launched into a discussion of the list she had given the man. But he wasn't listening. He started pacing back and forth between the living room and the kitchen, inspecting everything in his path with his hands. As far as he could tell, nothing else in the house had been disturbed by the visit.

"Forgive me, sweetheart," he said, sitting down beside her again. "It's all so new, it'll take me a while to get used to it." His hypocritical tone, which was lost on her, confused him a bit and at the same time gave him the reassurance that his rage, which he couldn't account for and yet carried inside him like a great weight, was something personal, nothing to do with her, something he could simply wish away at will.

It soon turned to summer. In the house in which he could move around freely but which pinned her down like a butterfly, the doors and windows were opened wide.

♪

At first he had no trouble conjuring up her image. Catlike eyes, small round mouth. When she was off on tour, as she so often was, he could also picture her performing on the stage. He knew the color of the dresses she wore — never black. Though her ivory arms moved without inhibition, she did her best to keep her face composed. The moment she was home again, those same facial features invariably got a little fuzzier, though in his excitement to have her all to himself again he didn't really care: at such moments his attention was focused mainly on her body. It was on one of these occasions that he grabbed her by the wrist and led her straight to the bedroom. She still had her coat on, and he was a bit nervous because she seemed different, not at all like the image he remembered from her voice and smell. But as soon as the door closed behind them, he calmed down, completely at ease. They were surrounded by inky darkness. Outside there was a brilliant October sun, and he knew it was a gorgeous day, but not one glint of light came into the room because three weeks ago she, Suzanna, had told him that she could actually only sleep well, sleep really deeply, in pitch blackness, so he had called a decorator. A heavy synthetic blackout curtain now lined the linen drapes, which meant that here, in the most intimate place in her house, she was stumbling around like a drunk and bumping into furniture. He bustled to and fro.

"Let me have your coat."

He helped her out of her coat.

"Take off your shoes."

He slipped her shoes off her feet.

It was as if the darkness had drugged her, as if its impenetrable depths had robbed her of her reason, so that he felt obliged, or perhaps took it upon himself, to help her out of her clothes, to throw back the covers, take her in his arms, and lay her down on the bed. It all seemed so perfect, as if the whole thing had been programmed. She lay as still as death, her arms and legs wondrously weightless as he lifted them up. The idea that the blind like to run their fingers over the faces and, if possible, the bodies of the people they meet in daily life is a myth. In reality, most blind people realize, just as normal people do, that the things you discover by touch — so very different from the things that are far away — should be kept in a category all their own.

His fingers explored the shapes, the surfaces, the recesses of her body. He knew he was doing something he had wanted to do for a long time. He turned her over on her stomach and later over on her back again. She said nothing, did nothing. He had persuaded her to let him look at her for his own enjoyment, as if by the light of a strong lamp, but without being disturbed by her watching eyes. By then they had been married for quite some time. Never before had he seen that she had such a beautiful body.

*H*e had stood facing the garden, trying to get himself under control. Behind him, the dinner conversation went on unabated. His sister Emily, with minimal support from her husband, was talking to Suzanna about her work.

"Marius?"

Her. Suzanna. He turned to the dining table and allowed his clenched fists in his trouser pockets to relax somewhat, though not completely. Ah, of course, she wants me to pass the bread basket, to taste the wine. This must have been during the second year of their marriage.

"Actually," Suzanna said, "if it weren't for him, we wouldn't be where we are now. He's the driving force behind the quartet. He works twenty-four hours a day and knows everything there is to know. Whether it's about an old disintegrating manuscript or the latest Kurtág, he has the answer."

He. She was talking about the Schulhoff Quartet's viola player.

Her voice changed. She was addressing him. "Well?"

Her hand on his wrist. He had swirled the Médoc around in his glass, brought it to his nose, and taken a sip.

"It's fine."

"Full of passion," Suzanna continued, to no one in particular. "A still water that runs very, very deep. Quite intriguing, even after all this time." And she adroitly held the glasses up to the bottle, one by one, so that their host was able to pour.

They did that often — invited friends and family to their home. He usually enjoyed those evenings; especially when the guests were people you could really talk to or laugh with, he would feel a tremendous sense of satisfaction in knowing that she, Suzanna, was at his side, and he would show her off the way you would a work of art, which, like every work of art, had a will of its own and was a distinct entity, something to be displayed as a favor to an intimate circle.

"Apparently I wasn't paying attention at your concert," the innocent Emily said to Suzanna. She was confusing the viola player with the stocky, curly-headed cellist.

"We know, now eat your dinner," he blurted out in irritation, to which his sister responded with an affectionate laugh, and her husband seemed to chortle. His brother-in-law Jacques, a contractor and real-estate developer, was a kindly man who said little except when the conversation revolved around the huge apartment complexes — "those silly high-rises," as Suzanna referred to them — that he was building up and down the coast.

"Oh, him!" Emily remembered when Suzanna began to describe the viola player. Tall, dark, glasses, high forehead, a face that looks serious, but . . .

Just when he noticed that she was sounding a bit breathless, her voice cracked and she broke off in mid-sentence. Coughing, she rushed over to the sink, though she did manage to squeeze out, "With dimples in his cheeks."

It was an incredibly revealing moment. He too lay down his knife and fork. For a few seconds he felt numb, and his hands sought the edge of the table. I'm an idiot, it dawned on him. An unsuspecting fool. Slowly, breathing deeply through his nose, he realized that nothing else would matter to him tonight now that the long-pent-up certainty in his chest had finally been blasted by the bombshell of a name. Good

God, Emile Bronckhorst, his wife's esteemed colleague! His fingers slid down the tablecloth, which reached to his knees. It was hard, starchy, and no doubt white, as spotlessly white as the truth.

"You look horrible," Emily cried when Suzanna, patting her chest with her hand, returned to the table.

Had his heinous deed actually been set in motion that night?

Soon afterward he had been too busy to devote much time to a personal matter of this kind. A trip to Los Angeles, a trip to New York, cities he knew well and where he had friends who helped him with his musicological research. No matter what time he called her from the Royal Shiba or the Sheraton, she was always at home. If he calculated, taking the time difference into account, that she would just be emerging from her morning shower, she would pick up the phone. If his 2:00 A.M. call woke her out of a deep sleep, she would first be alarmed, then greatly flattered that he simply wanted to hear her voice. With superhuman effort, he managed to forget that she rehearsed and performed several times a week with her quartet, and that a musician, as a person within a person, shares intimacies that others can't even begin to suspect.

After his return, he bombarded her for a while with semipolite, semiconfrontational questions about why she was late for dinner — tractors with protesting farmers had blocked the freeway — why she wasn't wearing her necklace — lost it — why the hell the living-room door had been left ajar so that he had bumped into it — she'd had a visitor — and at the beginning of spring their umpteenth conversation about the children he wanted her to have.

She said no. She said not yet. They continued to quarrel about it throughout the spring, though she repeatedly refused or else avoided the reproductive theme altogether by talking about next season's tour. It made him so miserable that once when they were standing on the little balcony at the top of the house, he took a step toward her and snarled in a loud whisper, "You want your freedom, huh?" He was filled with such anger that he felt the blood drain from his cheeks and the muscles of his face go slack.

Yes, she admitted without an ounce of sympathy, and she kept her trim figure for the rest of that year. And when she told him one afternoon in the following year that she was two months pregnant, the whole last year came rushing back to him, suddenly altered, like a landscape that looks different when you turn around to observe it from a distance than it did when you were walking through it one step at a time. It reduced his suspicions of the viola player, altered their squabbles about him, and simplified their frenzied reconciliations in bed, where his expressions of love had bordered on violence. "So this is what you've been after," she mumbled once, almost asleep.

One night, just as the year's first snow flurry began, the child came into the world quickly and without complications. He had been present at the birth. Using a stethoscope, he had been able to follow his son's exciting journey. When that remarkably light bundle was placed in his arms, neither the mother, the midwife, nor the nurse thought it the least bit odd that he repeatedly asked them to describe, in exact detail, what the newborn looked like. The visitors in the days to come also cooed convincingly: the baby had his father's blue eyes and the usual dark, downy hair that later turns blond.

*F*amilial bliss. Thanks to his memories, I could picture it clearly. Is there any man on earth who does not feel deeply touched when he sees his wife and son for the first time in the age-old pose of mother and child? It was cold that winter, van Vlooten told me. The garden froze; the nights were long. "I felt a serenity I had never before felt in my life."

We were still sitting side by side at the bar. I stretched my back, saw what he saw, but couldn't detach myself entirely from the unreal image the world was offering me. The airport was unusually crowded. Had more pilots gotten drunk? Looking around me at the endless number of passengers the two moving walkways were spewing forth, I was inclined to forgive any form of pilot protest.

"That's what you think," van Vlooten said in response to a lyrical comment of mine about marriage, and went on to tell me how he had personally done everything in his power to destroy that familial bliss and bring it to its unavoidable end.

For the rest, their household had run smoothly. They had hired a nursemaid, who also came over to babysit on the evenings Suzanna had to play. The chauffeur was initially a misunderstanding. The shy little man had actually been employed to curb Suzanna's freedom by driving her straight home after performances.

"How sweet of you!" She had thrown her arms around his neck, from where she was standing behind him. He could feel her soft wool sweater. "How thoughtful! I can barely resist the temptation!"

But she thought it was unnecessary, so the chauffeur and his Antillean wife moved into the cottage. It was the latter who planted the vegetable garden and occupied their kitchen two times a week to cook *pom, moksi metie, bakkeljauw,* and *kousenband,* Creole specialties that soon became their favorites.

"Would you do me a favor?" said van Vlooten, interrupting his own narrative.

"I'd be glad to."

"Order me a bottle of mineral water."

"A good idea. It's hotter than hell in here."

"I hardly noticed."

He still had on his blue raincoat. We drank in

silence. But the subject of our conversation soon came up again of its own accord.

"The problem is that her image, her portrait, began to fade."

"What!"

"It's not that unusual," he said, taking no notice of me. "Blind people who were once able to see forget what the people they live with look like. On the other hand, it takes only seconds to visualize someone you haven't seen for a while. Past acquaintances are stored in the archives of our memories with the sharpness of photographs."

"That makes sense. They haven't developed any further, which is why —"

"Yes, yes. That's it exactly," he interrupted. "So Suzanna, who ate at the same table with me every day, who drove me in the car, who slept with me, Suzanna's portrait got fuzzier and fuzzier and was finally on the verge of disappearing."

Suddenly upset, I picked up my glass. A gloomy thought had occurred to me, that no matter what you do or set out to do in life, it ultimately ends in emptiness and futility. I reminded van Vlooten of the conversation we had had ten years ago on the plane to Bordeaux, when he had claimed that God loved music, but not images — images that categorically deny time, after first greedily devouring it.

He listened to me in icy silence. He apparently didn't remember.

"And now," I continued angrily, "there's a backlash. Look what's happening now! The march of time is busy destroying the image!"

Van Vlooten didn't reply. After a while he turned to me.

"Do you want to hear something really strange? Sometimes when I tried to picture her, on one of those evenings when she was out, I didn't see her, but rather a painting that I saw long ago in Berlin." And he described the portrait of a woman with a chalky white face, a violet-blue hat on her head, sitting solemnly in the frontal pose of an underworld goddess, a Persephone, with her clamplike hands resting on the arms of a chair.

"That's possible," I replied indifferently.

♪

He hoped she would stop performing. He wanted her to have a couple more children. He asked her if she would have the decency to end her affair with the viola player, and he subsequently let the symptoms of an incipient madness, which he recognized as such at the time, grow unchecked. Once, during a violent gale, she had managed to lock herself in the storage shed next to the garage. She had a concert that evening. God knows what she had been looking for — he still had no idea, and it didn't matter — but the thing was, the wind had blown the door shut with such a bang that the flimsy doorknob had shot right out of the catch and fallen outside the shed.

When her voice finally reached him above the sound of the wind, he was sitting in his study at his typewriter. He instantly realized two things: She was in the storage shed, which was about six feet long and six feet wide with a trapdoor at the top, and she was upset by something, although it was hardly life-threatening. Anyway, he felt around for his shoes and walked to the back of the house, all the while thinking in spite of himself that his son and the nursemaid were not home. He paused in the kitchen doorway, twelve steps from the storage shed but in the howling wind, which was blowing her cries away from the cottage. Some ideas bore themselves into your brain like a red-hot poker. She had a concert that evening.

Perfect! At first, for the sheer pleasure of savoring his warped thoughts, of enjoying the twists and turns of his mind a while longer, he did nothing at all. How delightful it was to imagine the viola player stepping onto the stage tonight to offer his apologies and send the audience packing. To ensure that her cries for help would remain just that, he ambled back inside, went upstairs — the house was empty and smelled of freesias — and noticed how different the emptiness felt now than when she was absent in the usual way. The bathroom was in the middle of the house, so not a sound reached it from the outside. He turned on the water in the bathtub, laid out clean socks, underwear, and a new shirt, and undressed. He listened in carefree relaxation as the clock struck five-thirty, then six, and was just cutting his toenails when she burst in.

"You won't believe what happened to me!"

Oh, no?

She had fretted about tonight's concert for ages, she told him, before being rescued by the chauffeur's wife.

That same evening, at home, around eight-thirty, his hands started to shake, for no apparent reason. At that moment Suzanna was most certainly playing Mozart's K. 428, and she and the rest of the quartet had probably just reached the *andante con moto*. Softly but eloquently, he began to curse the walls of his house, those deadly silent witnesses to his isolated life, while just down the road she was being gaped at by an entire audience and leading a one-, two-, or even five-hundredfold existence. Peeping Toms, eyes squinting at a keyhole! Yes, but what could you do to stop it? Soon after that came a period in which he would arrive home from a short work-related trip to find that the furniture had been moved.

"Would *you* put up with that?" he asked me.

I told him of a case I'd heard about in Princeton,

my current place of residence, in which a man had sued for divorce and won because his obsessively energetic wife kept moving everything they owned, not just in the entire house, but also in their trailer.

"You see!" he said. "And he wasn't even blind!"

She denied it, of course. The supercilious maid swore up and down that the enormous William and Mary desk had always stood on that spot, and the same was true of the sofa. . . . "Stop it or else!" Suzanna tore her arm out of his grasp. They had fought for days simply because she refused to admit something he had been absolutely sure of for years. Neither of them, by the way, mentioned the viola player by name on such occasions. The name Emile Bronckhorst referred simply and solely to her colleague in the Schulhoff Quartet, the man whose hand he went backstage to shake, like all the others, after the first performance of every new program.

"What did you think of it, Marius?" the viola player asked him at the end of a combined Schubert and Schoenberg concert. The two men began to talk about how amazingly well the two composers went together in a program.

"Both rebels," van Vlooten remarked.

"Indeed," the other agreed. "Both brave enough to do without historical support if they have to."

Their voices met at the same height, since the viola player was also tall, with a heavy build.

"Shall we go?" Suzanna asked him after a while, and he followed her to the side exit, which opened onto the nighttime parking lot. Because he wasn't used to their new car yet, she placed his hand on the open door so he could find his seat, then got in herself. They drove out of the city and turned toward the coast.

"Did you think," van Vlooten asked me after a brief silence, "or do you perhaps assume that a blind man, unlike everyone else, doesn't seek a demon for his stress? Ulcers, eczema, alcoholism, mental illness . . . ?" He brought his hands to his temples, as if to say: But why, for heaven's sake, in my case *this?*

"My jealousy," he said slowly — and it was the first time I'd heard him use the word — "my jealousy tore apart our love, which was bound by a thousand and one things, and turned it into a swarm of angry hornets."

They drove into the village and at the traffic circle took the road toward the sea. Suzanna was silent, concentrating on her driving, and since there was a treacherous rise, it was just as well. All of a sudden he started shouting that he couldn't stand it anymore, that they had gone too far, she and her lover. Furious, he demanded to know whether her paramour managed, in their various hotel beds, to satisfactorily perform the special, sleepy-eyed variation on the *combat amoureux* that she liked so much, particularly early in the morning!

Ignoring his crassness, she drove up the drive-way toward the garage, the doors of which opened automatically onto a brightly lit interior.

"Don't make such an ugly face," she said. He got out of the car without waiting for her.

As he entered the kitchen, he bumped his head on the hanging lamp. He opened the refrigerator, but the gin wasn't in its usual place. On the stairs he tripped over a pair of shoes. Hoping to find out if his son was home, he went in to give him a good-night kiss, but only after he had wandered through the babysitter's room did he finally stumble into the child's bed, pushed up against the wall, next to a dresser. In the master bedroom, he quickly undressed and was already in bed by the time he heard her switch on the light. She lay down beside him. Not until he heard the light click again did he turn onto his side so that he was facing her, as he normally did.

♪

We stepped onto the moving walkway. Our flight had been announced, so we were heading for Gate G86 in a remote corner of the airport. Van Vlooten remained standing behind me while a procession of Jesus freaks passed us on the left, walking briskly by in their san-dals. I glanced over my shoulder and was once more shocked by his face. He looks as though he's had a stroke, I thought, and from my close vantage point observed the drooping corner of his mouth, which was wet. Is this what she had meant by "an ugly face"? How awful it must be not to have the faintest idea of your own facial expression.

"It's still insanely busy," I reported.

Van Vlooten didn't react, clearly unwilling to let his thoughts stray from where they were. Fine, I also cast my mind back, to when he was trying to hide his face from her — all very understandable — but the erotic plight that popped into my head was the amusing tale of Cupid and Psyche, the couple who could only make love in the dark because she, the poor dear, wasn't allowed to know her husband's true identity.

"The walkway's coming to an end," I warned.

He grunted, stuck out his arms, and took a giant step. In the time it took for us to move on to the next walkway and for me to look back and see if he was all right, my mind had shifted to less rosy literature.

"The soul is a terrible reality. . . . It can be poisoned, or made perfect."

With my hand on the sticky rail of the slow-moving walkway, I ruminated on Dorian Gray, the doomed man who was forced to hide the oil portrait of himself behind a curtain in an unused room, who couldn't show the masterly painting to anyone else because an all-too-human element had crept in. While he himself stayed as beautiful as spring and as young as a colt, the portrait took on his loathsome life, its face mercilessly reflecting his every transgression. Well, from there it was a small mental leap to the red-carpeted classroom in Bordeaux one morning many years ago, when the affable Eugene Lehner had leaned over a score and, only after a prolonged silence, made a remark. What had he been staring at during those moments of silence?

I'm not going to ask him, I thought. I'm not going to ask the bent, broken man behind me whether he ever again heard his wife play that quartet, the master-piece composed by that sensitive skeptic, that way-ward modernist Janáček, who, like many of his fellow composers, put things in his music that were meant not only for the listening ear but also for the inner eye — in other words, the story. Consequently, in bars 1–45 of the first movement, anyone who wishes to can clearly visualize a beautiful woman. She is married. In the second movement, the *con moto*, with all those ominous tremolos, we can picture her meeting an elegant gentleman, bars 1–47, who also happens to be an excellent violinist. Flirtation: bars 48–67; sugges-tive remarks: bars 68–75; the encounter appears to be far from innocent: bars 185–224. Then comes the third movement, catastrophic from beginning to end, when we realize that the power of music is not always inno-cent, especially not when one is playing Beethoven, bars 8–10.

And another piece? As we stepped off the walkway and van Vlooten put his hand on my shoulder, I was still pondering the third movement, particularly the racing thirty-second notes of the *sčasovka*, a motif you run into often in Janáček. All well and good, but in this case, bars 1–34, that sweet little ditty is used to represent the demon, the evil spirit who manages, with spectacular success, to drive the husband mad. The master of the house, an inherited character who is very nasty indeed, falls into the clutches of jealousy.

Surely, I thought as I trundled along with the blind man half a step behind me, he must have heard that piece many times before, since it was popular with musicians and audiences alike. But there, in Bordeaux, it had grabbed him by the shoulders and spun him around for twenty minutes, until he no longer knew where he was. Being the person you think you are, yet finding yourself standing in front of a strange door . . .

Increasing madness — the third movement races on. Quarrel: bar 35. Lament: bars 39–59. The andante is a breather of sorts, but there's no getting around the score, so with a heavy heart, bars 60–70, the woman admits to herself that she would be delighted if a certain fantasy, bars 73–88, were to come true. In the fourth movement one thing after another goes terribly wrong.

Quite literally, yes. But works of art meet and part. Brno, the autumn of 1923. Janáček is sitting at a wobbly table that he's tried to fix by shoving a folded piece of paper under one of the legs. He's working on a composition inspired by Tolstoy's *Kreutzer Sonata*, the novella that excites him, annoys him, and no doubt intrigues him greatly. For almost twenty years he's been carrying the lovesick, jealousy-ridden characters around in his head, and the composer in him has toyed with the idea before. Now, in just eight days, he jots down what he has to say. Everything immediately falls into place. The composer, at the age of almost seventy, gives a new twist to the spiral of passion and fate that has gone from sonata to novella to string quartet.

After writing down the four bars of the maestoso, he doesn't pause, but goes on working — almost unconsciously, not looking back — until it's time for dinner. A few days later he lays down his pencil, then leafs slowly through the music, rubs his face, and sits for a long time without moving. Being whoever you want to be, in moments of intense concentration, without ever being entirely free of the other person you are as well. Was it the space between these two, the wellspring of a work of art, that Eugene Lehner had been staring at, back then, in Bordeaux?

♪

A female voice on the loudspeaker announced our flight to Salzburg for the second time. That always makes you hurry, but we made little headway in the crowded corridor. Rather unexpectedly, we spotted a sign for G86 with an arrow pointing down. After a short flight of steps, we found ourselves in a surprisingly quiet room, where the passengers for Salzburg and Bucharest were waiting for the bus that would take them to the plane. We sat down. As I was catching my breath I had the feeling that van Vlooten's hand was still resting on my shoulder, that's how heavily he had leaned on me at the end.

"Are you sure you want this infernal topic of conversation to continue?" he asked. His voice was calm, but the look on his face seemed to say: Don't you dare stop me now!

"I'm listening," I said.

*I*t happened on the train. Suzanna, sitting across from him, reported that they were passing through green fields and banks full of poppies and cornflowers. They had stayed with friends in Brussels, had spent a quiet lunch hour with these same friends in the station restaurant, and were now on their way home. Under the deceptive influence of the train's rhythm, the conversation turned to marital problems — specifically those of Emily and the real-estate developer — and they began talking in low voices about a fling his sister had had.

"Goodness," Suzanna said at a certain moment. "You're certainly getting all worked up over this." And then, swallowing a yawn: "That kind of thing happens in the best of marriages, doesn't it?"

As in a trance, he heard himself agree. He shifted in his seat, laughed when she teasingly asked him something, and admitted, as in a trance, "Yes, of course." And then, in response to another question, he told Suzanna about a trifling episode involving an English woman whom he had met a year or so ago at the *Spiegel der Musikkritik* symposium in Munich. Needless to say, he and Suzanna were going through another one of those periods in which they were making love to each other frequently and passionately, which always brought them closer together.

"Marius!" Suzanna reacted in a supposedly shocked tone of voice, and he grinned, leaving aside for the moment the question of whether the cheerful stab of guilt he felt was for her, the broad-minded Suzanna, or for the scholarly young woman whose sumptuous curves he briefly thought back to with great pleasure.

The compartment shook. "Flanders is so beautiful," Suzanna said. Dangerously continuing their chat, she in turn confessed a misdeed in her own past.

He pretended he wasn't listening.

As if delighted to be able to finally pour out her feelings, to tell the truth at last since it probably did a marriage a world of good, all the more so if your husband couldn't see, she told him several fairly precise details about her long-ago tour to Israel. He shut his eyes. Let his head droop. An adoring fan, a nice young man with access to a beach cabin in Eilat. She giggled. He decided to think of something else — the real-estate developer came to mind — and started breathing slowly and heavily, the way people do before they doze off. And while he gently snored and pictured his brother-in-law's latest, not yet completed "composition in concrete and sandstone," eight stories high, an imaginative layout, and thought about its main attraction, the view of the North Sea, her chatter died down. Hmm, her husband was taking a nap, not a bad idea, and he heard her slip off her shoes and make room for her legs on the seat.

It must have been about two weeks before the murder attempt. There she sat, peacefully asleep in a compartment that was empty except for the two of them. Though she didn't realize it, she was sitting across from a maniac, a man bursting with the kind of restless energy that always finds an outlet. When the conductor slid open the door, he was the one who handed over the tickets. Only when they were coming into the Hollands Spoor station in The Hague did he tap her knee. "We're here." As they climbed into the cab, he thought, quite calmly and with a feeling of total reasonableness, I want her out of my life, and he gave the driver their address.

A vague wish, hardly more than a fantasy. Which path does a possibility have to take before becoming a decision? The alarm clock went off at six-forty-five the next morning. He had had an excellent night's sleep. He took a shower while she lay in bed a bit longer, and as he stood under the steaming jets of water, five minutes of hot followed by a final blast of cold, his state of mind was hardly any different than usual. As he mulled over his plans for the day, he also mulled over another plan, a scheme that may have passed into the realm of madness during the night, but that now struck him as the conclusion, short but definite, to an ingenious line of reasoning.

With malice aforethought. Which is said to be the most terrible of the most terrible of acts.

"It is, isn't it?"

Van Vlooten mumbled as he asked me the question, but pointed his chin at the weary row of passengers across from us as if to say: Don't contradict me!

I looked away from him, into the waiting room, where the strange silence was broken only by a Slovakian knocking the ashes off his pipe by tapping it against the window frame.

"Oh, well," I said. "What's the difference? Between the carefully planned crime and the it-went-dark-before-my-eyes variety? In my opinion they both stem from the same raging fury."

He didn't react to my remark. Not even when I added, "Anyway, isn't long-term madness more surreptitious, more tempting, even more sensible?"

He had sat down at the breakfast table. The sun had shone on his hands through the window. His son had come downstairs, followed by Suzanna, who put the bread in the toaster, scooped the eggs out of the frying pan, poured the tea. While he chatted with the little six-year-old boy as usual, the normal day-to-day things fell into place again and revolved around two highly relevant questions: when and how?

Out on the driveway their two cars, parked by the chauffeur, were ready to go, with Suzanna's in front. Her quartet always rehearsed in Voorburg, at the viola player's house, since it was the most accessible of the four.

♪

"Do you think I cared? No, there was no need to give it any special thought or to waste another word on the matter. She had been cheating on me for years; it couldn't have been easier or more convenient, with our good friend from the Schulhoff Quartet, the ensemble to which she had already dedicated her life. Of course I know she hasn't admitted it and that it can't be proven, that my position is based on conjecture, a diabolical fever, but that doesn't make it any less true. The scenes my wife took part in were not just a figment of my imagination, but were played on a real stage, among the shifting furniture in our house and our oh-so-flexible friends!"

Not long afterward, one night when his brother-in-law was expounding on the high-rises along the coast again, he became so interested that he asked him if he could view one sometime. "Don't laugh.

Over the years lots of blind people have developed a highly subtle, specialized sensitivity to walls, corridors, and ceilings, which they 'see' with their ears rather than their eyes by listening to the acoustics bounce back. They appreciate buildings as much as architects do."

So the next day, a cool Tuesday morning, he had the chauffeur drop him off at the construction site. "Come back in twenty minutes," he told him. "I'm bound to be done by then."

He had paused for a moment, registering the chaos — a radio was playing somewhere — when footsteps came thumping across the planks and a voice shouted hello. His brother-in-law greeted him and clasped his outstretched hand.

"Follow me. The elevators are over here."

"No," he replied, "I'll take the stairs."

The other man seemed to understand that a visually challenged person such as he would prefer to sense the building's height, all eight concrete floors, as physically as possible.

A six- or seven-minute climb. He stood, gasping for breath, on the flat roof of the highest apartment. Dizzy from lack of oxygen, he heard the sound of the pounding surf rise up mightily and mingle with his thoughts.

"The most beautiful view, in fact the only pure, unadulterated view of nature we still have in this

country," exclaimed his brother-in-law, likewise panting, behind him. "Water, clouds, a magnificent boat on
the horizon!"

"Oh, really?" he replied, thinking: Keep your
sales pitch to yourself. I'm fully capable of thinking
up reasons why Suzanna might be prepared to live in
this light, spacious penthouse.

The cry of a seagull. The wind in his face, an
invisible whip, which to a sighted person could never
have quite the same saltiness or tingly sensation,
which could evoke the strangest of memories, such as
now, for example, amid all else, Suzanna's voice, first
seductively describing what she was taking off (her
dress, her stockings), then what she still had on (pale
green, expensive silk), for she was a woman with a
great need to be found beautiful.

"Shall I tell you what kept running through my
head all that day and the next?"

"I think I can imagine," I said evasively.

"Well, what concerned me most were the meas-
urements and location of the rooftop patio. I had
carefully tapped it out with my cane, right up to the
edge, though my brother-in-law was having a fit because the balustrade, made of imported green Cararra
marble, hadn't been put up yet."

Suzanna had a few days off just then, which gave
him time to calmly describe the seaside penthouse,
get her used to the idea of a change in their lives, and

make her curious enough to want to go with him and have a look. His brother-in-law had given him the blueprints. "Great big sheets of paper," van Vlooten told me, and he confessed to taking particular delight in spreading them out on his desk and having Suzanna describe them to him.

She had leaned over his shoulder.

"A living room that's twenty feet wide and twenty-six feet deep," she said pensively.

She rested her left hand on the back of his chair, and with her right hand traced the black rectangular lines. Her chest pressing lightly into his back, she said, "A patio with sliding doors across the entire length."

What was going through his mind at the time?

"Don't try to understand," van Vlooten said. Whenever he was home during the next couple of days, he calmly made meticulous preparations for what he thought of as a challenge, difficult but not impossible, a subtle task that a man ought to be able to carry out in his lifetime. Suzanna, who was in and out a lot, kept interrupting him. Actually, during that final phase he had no desire to talk to her, which made her mad, so that one day she stood in the hall outside his study and screamed at him, demanding that he say something, until he finally got up angrily from his desk, walked over to her, stopped for a moment to light a cigarette, slammed the door in her face, then promptly went back to concentrating on a deed he didn't think of for a moment as real, but that was nevertheless an interesting and relaxing exercise.

"So that's what was going through my mind," van Vlooten said. "As long as I was in my own house, the whole business felt like an exercise, a score with no indication of which instruments were to be played, a piece that was never meant to be performed."

Suddenly the corner of his mouth twitched violently. But whenever he found himself on the eighth floor, after another climb up those diabolical stairs, which he climbed twice that last week, he felt such a rage that he decided to finish what he had begun.

That Thursday evening, Suzanna was sitting in the sunroom, gabbing away on the phone. It was one of those endless conversations of hers with someone from the quartet. He didn't care who it was. When she hung up, he said, "Let's talk." She stood up, walked across the living room, and reluctantly sat down beside him on the couch. Filled with an utterly impersonal thrill at the thought of a deed that was so far advanced it was all but committed, he asked her if she felt like going with him tomorrow morning to look at the apartment.

He had gone by briefly that afternoon just to make sure. The sun had been shining; there had been a slight breeze. The chauffeur had dropped him off, and he had managed to find the stairwell on his own — he no longer needed his brother-in-law. Tense, absolutely focused, he had mounted the stairs with a studied look of indifference on his face because he could sense the presence of the construction workers, who had gotten to know him during the last few weeks. He reached the top with the stench of concrete in his nostrils and his heart pounding in his chest, but with every one of his senses alive, so alive that he thought: Suzanna, I'll be damned. For there was her face, more striking than he had ever pictured it before, her nearly erased portrait restored, and he envisioned her entire figure, dressed in dazzling yellow, just as it had been one summer day when she had looked away from a babbling crowd of cocktail drinkers and turned her full face toward his. Shedding reality. Such moments are fleeting, and are usually followed by an anguished emptiness. In trying to find the elevator, he first shuffled off in the wrong direction, but finally found the buttons and rode down through the skeletal frame of the unfinished building, through the construction noise, the pounding, the drilling, and from somewhere a hollow, windborne shout that may have been a greeting.

She was silent, in an all-too-familiar form of sulking protest.

"The penthouse, you mean," she finally said.

"Yes," he said.

He could feel her hesitate. The tension in their house had been unbearable lately.

"Fine."

bus drove up to the plate-glass door. At the same moment two airline employees sauntered over to the counter. Everyone started moving. Van Vlooten stretched himself to his full height, nearly losing his balance. I pressed his cane into his hand. It was still quite hot, I noticed when we went outside. The asphalt glared, the bus gave off waves of shimmering heat. Van Vlooten tripped on his way in, and someone immediately offered him a seat. The bus took off with a sharp turn. Though I had braced myself in the aisle, I almost fell on top of my companion. His upper lip was beaded with sweat. I thought to myself: Anyone who goes to such great lengths is bound to carry out his plan. . . . It was cool in the plane. We took off to an orchestral arrangement of Schubert's "Wohin So Schnell," accepted a glass of kirsch, and abandoned ourselves to the sudden acceleration, the upward thrust, and the pressure in the cabin, which may seem natural, but isn't, and can make anyone who's sensitive to it feel light-headed. Van Vlooten leaned toward me. "I can tell you this," he said, his voice high, hoarse, subdued. "I woke up that morning feeling extraordinarily well-rested."

He was breathing heavily.

*I*t was a beautiful May morning. The first one out of bed as usual, he drew the heavy drapes back from the windows, which had been open all night, so that he could sniff the garden, still damp but already slightly warmed by the sun, and farther away, the sandy smell of the dune that was blocking the gentle slap of the waves because there wasn't a breath of wind today. All very familiar, known to him since the day he was born, and he paused for a few minutes to savor the mystery of it, of the moment when what has been lets you know that it is shifting, irrevocably, into what will be. Was this fate?

And did fate appear twenty minutes later in the guise of a woman, a man, and a little boy at a breakfast table? Perhaps, or perhaps half of it did, while the other half consisted of your heart, contracting, filling with blood, beating steadily on.

"Why aren't you eating?" said Suzanna, who was never chatty in the morning, by way of greeting.

Pretending not to have heard her, he dutifully asked his son, "What did you dream about last night, Benno?" The child promptly started telling him something that didn't interest him at all, but made him think with a kind of dizziness: Soon! Soon everything, organized down to the last detail, will have settled down again!

He stood up, coffee cup in hand, forefinger crooked over the edge so he could gauge the liquid inside. Very slowly, as if he were already resting from something he had not yet done but had vowed to do, he walked through the open door and out to the patio bordering the row of flowers in the vegetable garden.

"I'm not eating because I'm not hungry!"

Leaning against the wall in the sun, he thought: Okay, we're already up, breakfast is nearly over, and if Suzanna would hurry up and take the child to school, it would be more than welcome. Feeling his wristwatch with his fingers, he spilled coffee all over his hand. He quickly drank the rest, put the cup down by his foot, yawned, and had to force himself not to yawn again. His eyes filled with tears. So this is how a disastrous day begins, he mused, though nothing has happened yet and everything is going peacefully as usual, following its natural inclination and not the viselike madness that makes a person concentrate on the vilest, most twisted part of himself.

She honked the horn at nine-fifteen when she returned from the school and let the engine run. He climbed in. "Take a hard right at the end of Wassenaarseweg. You know where I mean," he said, with his back pressed to the seat, his head tilted forward, listening, following the familiar curves in the road. Only after she had merely muttered "Okay" to several of his directions and made a mistake by the Dunes Hotel, of all places, so that she had to turn around, did he finally realize that she wasn't listening all that carefully to him because she was distracted by something.

"You ought to be able to see the building from here!"

This was it. She parked on the iron sheeting that had been laid down on the building site to facilitate driving. A clear blue sky and seagulls again, he surmised as they left the car. And about fifty yards away a pounding crane with a clanging hook. It would be a while before anyone would be able to hear the sea.

"Come on."

He led her, cane tapping, into the foyer, which was drafty since there were still no doors and windows. Why didn't she protest? Why didn't she suggest that they take the elevator? He trudged up the first flight of stairs with the measured tread of someone who knows the route over which he has to pace himself. Without turning to look at her — why bother? — he babbled something about the projected completion date, but fell silent when there was no response from her. On the second and third flights it was so quiet behind him that he had the feeling he was alone, that the whole enterprise had tricked him and decided, on second thought, to remain what it had been up to now, an idea that drove you stark raving mad. He grabbed the railing. His sweaty palm slipped off. But on the fourth floor, where he stopped for a minute by a ladder and a couple of cans of paint, he heard her panting, softly but clearly. At that moment it struck him: she feels it, she feels that something is happening, already this place has her in its thrall, and the danger, which she doesn't quite grasp so that it's even more intriguing, is luring her with its enormous powers of persuasion closer and closer with every step she takes.

They climbed higher. Over the last flight of stairs lay a tangled mass of telephone or electricity cables, wires that would connect the future residents to the world. He picked his way around them, his footsteps echoing in the empty space, hers inaudible. He shook his head, dizzy. Oh, it was because of her, because of her paralyzingly acquiescent behavior, that their climb, their breathing, their silence, was beginning to take on the dangerous, unreal power of a ceremony.

He was now longing for the platform in the open air. The cold draft rising up through the stairwell bothered him. Besides, he had the oddest feeling that she was the one who couldn't see a hand in front of her face, that she was having to make a tremendous effort not to lose him in the dark. He counted the steps. Concentrate, don't think. Moments like these are not for thought, but for memory and a vivid imagination.

Her everyday behavior. Her clothes. Her smell. Her good moods and her bad moods. Her voice, the compass by which he could always find her, the permanent north in an otherwise changing world. She had cut off her braid a while ago, and now wore her hair down around her shoulders. Her soothing convictions, her descriptive talents, her curiosity. The sensual mind of a creature who was used to curling up comfortably beside him on the sofa late at night. Since the birth of their son, she had gotten a bit broader in the hips, but her ankles were still no wider than his wrists. Her marathon phone calls. Her hearty laugh among friends: she was a woman who rarely, if ever, cried. Her parties. Her afternoons with the child. The evenings they went out together, and his swooning intoxication, already in the car, from the perfume on her neck. Her musicality. He had often heard her practicing on the top floor of the house, the sound of her violin going right through the floorboards, mournful, dynamic, *largamente*. If he raised his head to listen, he would realize that he was far away from her, farther away than her violin case, her music stand, her sheet music, and her scores, which she would pore over, pencil poised, as she sat in the glow of the table lamp.

All of this he remembered, a sharp, joyful image, accompanied by an inner voice that said: Not long! And so he came to the last step, where he could already smell the thin salty air of the roof. Keyed to a fever pitch, long on the verge of a nervous breakdown, he didn't feel a single doubt, for her infidelity was a fact, though the pain was not as great as it had once been.

His foot landed with a plop on the floor tiles. He had miscalculated the number of steps.

"We're here," he said.

"You're shaking all over," she said with a sigh.

♪

He heard her walk through the empty rooms. The blueprints still fresh in her mind, she inspected and mentally furnished the "living area," the "multipurpose room," the "kitchen," the "bathroom," and the "auxiliary space" without saying a word, for which he was grateful. He waited. Standing on the patio next to the wide-open sliding door, he listened to see if she would step into the apartment's chief inducement, the "outside area."

He barely gave her a thought. He certainly didn't think of her as a woman turning her head this way and that, or standing still, or narrowing her eyes to examine the house she might possibly live in, while in the back of her head she had already formed an idea, despite her strange mood, of how the rest of her day would go. Inconceivable to him. Just as her silk slacks, loose and sporty, with pockets that buttoned below the knee, her suede shoes, and her soft T-shirt were totally inconceivable to him now that she had become, except for that one final movement, what she would always be from now on: futureless.

He heard the sea rush out — it was low tide. And the roar of what was probably the beach police's jeep heading slowly north, then dying away. While continuing to track her position to within a margin of error of a step or two, he didn't feel the slightest hesitation. On the contrary, there was still one act he had to perform, and its magical power was so great that he could feel it as a kind of firm authoritarian resolve in the muscles of his arms. In such cases it is no longer a question of wanting to or not wanting to, of yes or no. After all, he had already proven once before that he could heed the siren call of death, that at a given moment he was capable of saying, "Now."

She strolled toward the patio, but then stopped at the threshold. Had she glanced at the sea and become absorbed, as everyone invariably does, by that infinite, everlasting stretch of water and sky? At this hour of the day the sea was a shade darker than the sky; when dusk fell, it would be the other way around. He said nothing, nor did he beckon her, but clenched his jaw, stretched out his arm, tapped his cane with extra emphasis, took the few steps to the place where he was going to push her, accurate to within an inch, and listened. She followed him, like an animal that suddenly stops running from danger, only to turn and face it head on, so inextricably is the animal bound to its fate.

And so she came to stand in her spot. Unseen, unheard. Yet he knew that together he and she had now assumed that one inexorable position, of trigger and target, which is the equivalent of a command. Concentrating every fiber of his being, he took a breath.

There he was, in a sunny open space. Down below, the construction workers were taking their nine-thirty coffee break in a shed. And as for his heart, well, at that moment there was scarcely a personal emotion in it. Yes, that's how it was: a highly abstract moment in which he felt free, infinitely free to do something that no one would ever find out about. What's the truth about a secret, a carefully guarded secret? How long can it remain intact before it starts showing signs of a feature that has characterized it from the beginning — falsehood? It can happen in a flash. You are what you do; yes, perhaps we are. But an act in a permanent state of concealment can vanish from your life with surprising swiftness, because there's no one to blame you.

He was surprised by a sound. Suzanna, a mere hand's breadth away, took a deep breath, every bit as deep as his, and for one absurd moment he thought: She's going to sneeze! She's going to have one of those strange sneezing fits of hers!

The moment passed. She backed away. He heard a few cautious steps. Already the entire constellation, perfect down to the last inch, had shifted, moved impossibly far apart, and the world had wriggled out of his grasp. He didn't move, just turned his head. She had stopped at the threshold between the living room and the patio, and he knew, with absolute certainty, that they were now looking straight at each other's faces — his with a scowl of admission that would always be his true face, hers so ruthlessly perceptive that she could no doubt hear him think: I wish you were dead! Dead!

He heard her race through the living room toward the stairs.

16

es, she did take the stairs."

Van Vlooten opened his mouth wide, which struck me, still dazed by the events I had just heard, as such a macabre thing to do that I thought: He's not going to make it! A moment later, however, I too felt a painful pressure on my eardrums. The plane had begun its rapid descent.

"Salzburg!" I said, with a glance at my watch. It was eleven-twenty.

Van Vlooten sat up straight. "She raced toward the stairs," he resumed. "And I'm fairly certain that she ran down all seven flights, which from her point of view I can certainly understand."

I intimated that I understood it too. Step after step, I thought, at her own speed and on her own two feet, of course, and meanwhile very much aware of the widening gap between him and her, between the threat

of scandal above and her sprinting self, a dead and
resurrected spirit, rummaging around for her car keys.

"How did you get home?" I asked solicitously.

It hadn't been easy. By the time he had made his
way downstairs, van Vlooten told me, the construction site had been transformed into a silent ghost
town. He took a wrong turn on the sandy plain, lost
his cane, and bumped into the shed by sheer accident,
but the place was deserted. After stumbling around in
the hot sun for a while, he managed to reach the road,
where finally, after a long wait, a German tourist picked
him up. And so he arrived home, too tired to think
and too afraid to go in. He waited at the foot of the
driveway, supporting himself with one hand on the
mailbox, which had a newspaper jutting out of it.
Soon he realized that the two cars were parked on the
gravel drive with their doors open. He registered the
sound of footsteps, but no voices. Shortly afterward
the doors slammed shut. The engines revved into life.

"They drove right past me," van Vlooten said, in
a voice that made no attempt to hide his sorrow. "The
gravel bounced against my feet, and reason descended
on me again with the swiftness of a guillotine. Realizing full well that I had destroyed my life, I retreated to
the low wooden fence."

We had landed. As I handed him his raincoat
from the overhead compartment, van Vlooten said,
"My, aren't you a good boy." And in the arrival hall,

he asked me what time it was. "Almost midnight," I said, while ruefully observing how we, fellow travelers who had reached our destinations, were busy distancing ourselves from one another. After I had grabbed his suitcase from the baggage-claim belt for him, he started to walk away, one step ahead of me. Knowing that he was going to be picked up by a friend, I thought, well, that's that, but then he, the blind giant, turned around by the passport-control gate and startled the entire line of passengers by coming to a halt and rolling his eyes.

"Excuse me. Sorry. *Entschuldigung!*" I mumbled.

I pushed my way to the front.

"Farewell," I said. And I shook his hand, which felt stiff and cold.

Sixteen Years Later

*O*ne winter's day, a Saturday, toward the end of November. For years I had hardly given the two of them a thought, but on that day I would accidentally hear the end of their story. Unconsciously I had always assumed that I had seen the end with my own eyes, so hopeless and heartbreaking had it been to watch the music critic stride through customs in Salzburg, not so much aged as desperately lost and damaged by life. From that moment on, my image of Suzanna Flier was no longer compatible with that of this difficult and also handicapped man, and I automatically assumed that the ambitious friend of my conservatory days was touring the musical stages of Europe with her quartet and taking loving care of her little boy.

I was living in Boston at the time. I had been invited to attend a seminar, Music for Eyes and Ears, in Wiesbaden, to hold a series of guest lectures in Paris on Janáček and his fascination with the death of his heroines, and, first of all, to give a talk in Amsterdam titled "Orpheus's Backward Glance: An Accident?" Accordingly, on that cold, clear morning I took a cab to the airport so that I could fly from Logan Airport to Schiphol, and halfway through the flight, so unexpectedly that it took my breath away, I came across the names of Marius van Vlooten and his wife, Suzanna Flier, and was shocked into silence.

The main theme of their beautiful and horrific tale did not appear to be the one that my memory had long ago circled in red.

For I don't claim that this couple didn't occupy my thoughts for a while. That they didn't continue to haunt me until I had filed them in the domain from which I believe they came. After all, art is one of this society's chief preoccupations, isn't it? All those civilizations, all those revolutions, all those achievements: surely there's no harm in wondering every now and then about the how and the why? Without Homer, no Shackleton, I once mused in connection with an existence that exists in a chillingly beautiful décor but is hardly capable of imagining anything on its own. And so my interest again turned to Marius van Vlooten and Suzanna Flier and to the various stages of their fate. When van Vlooten and I passed through Austria's customs on that long-ago night, we were both tired.

We heard a horn honking outside, we heard people talking and shouting, and above it all we heard that eternal female voice booming over the loudspeaker in the arrival hall, addressing us on the theme of eroticism, madness, compassion, and the moment of despair when a couple realizes that it's better to separate for good.

Sunny, but cold. The young cabdriver, ignoring the wheels under my suitcase, lifted it with ease and led the way. As he swung open the rear door, I saw him glance at the book I held. It was a Turkish novel in an English translation, a thick volume that would help me while away the six hours on the plane and transport me into a totally different world. We drove off. My eyes met those of the driver in the rearview mirror. I had the feeling that he wanted to say something, but changed his mind when he noticed that I had opened my book. After a quiet ride, in which we didn't exchange a word, we reached the airport.

"That silent house," the young man said, as he extended the handle on my suitcase. "I still dream about it sometimes."

In the departure lounge I realized just how sensible it had been to bring along a book that already had me under its spell. According to the monitor, my flight had been delayed, and further inquiries revealed that KL 218 was one of many planes waiting to have its wings de-iced. During the next hour and a half, I didn't notice a thing: I read. By the time we finally boarded, I barely recognized my surroundings, because I was completely wrapped up in the melancholy of that nearly deserted house, the Turkish one in my book. The fact remains, however, that out of the 465 passengers that can be seated in a Boeing 747, I wound up in the middle of the row, in the least comfortable seat, and that three of those 465 passengers formed a garrulous group of friends, with two on my right and one on my left.

Newspapers were being distributed. I grabbed one. "European Army a Pipedream," "China Promises to Improve Record," "Money-Laundering Affair in Holland," "Tuberculosis in Russia," "Housing Market Skyrockets," "Sperm Cells to Become Obsolete," "Soccer Sponsors Demand More Goals," "Chirac Admonishes Americans," *"Ulysses* Manuscript Sold for $1.5 Million," "Dioxin Found in Eels" ... The stuff of real life, not a theory. As the plane started to climb, I stared at the headlines, which bore no relation at all to the drama and events in my head nor to any meaningful logic I could think of. In the meantime the plane had reached its cruising altitude, and the friends on either side of me had started to converse. Because I was pretty much of an obstacle, they had to speak rather loudly to make themselves heard, but when I offered to change places, they said, "What for?" So I couldn't help observing that the two women, who had the trendy TV jargon down pat, were obsessed with the idea that sexual relationships were supposed to be fun, varied, and problem-free, and that the young man occasionally disagreed.

"It's funny," the brunette on my right, who was wearing a short, loose-fitting skirt over a pair of pants, said, for example, to the young blond, leaning slightly forward, on my left. "In the relationships I've had up to now, I was the one who was always compromising, I mean, God was I ever impressed with Mr. Big, but now I just think, wow, cute guy, a real teddy bear, but ... does he meet my needs?"

The blond ran her hand through her sleek hair, hanging down on either side of her head like a curtain, leaned forward even more, and only then replied with a sideways glance, "Yeah, I'm also tired of all that symbiosis, that round-the-clock togetherness. I like men, but from now on my days and nights belong to *me.* I was in a relationship for six years. He bought me Coco Chanel and washed the windows of our apartment every other Saturday. But my positive feelings went into a nosedive and I felt like, you know, is this all there is? In terms of sex, I thought, I'm not getting all that much out of it, and yet I was still hanging on to the guy. Anyway, I've got a decent income. So I could afford to call it quits."

I reclined my seat. An inexplicable sadness began to steal over me. The reddish glow of twilight had already appeared outside the windows. A flight attendant with an inconsolable smile was walking languidly up and down the aisles, passing out hot towels with a pair of tongs. Now it was the turn of the young man, who was sitting the farthest from me, to proffer his theory of love and fidelity. He argued that eroticism, true eroticism, is monogamous because sexual desire is concentrated on one object, like a burning glass converging the rays of the sun to a single point, but the two women stared at him and knitted their brows as if they were deep in thought. They only came to life again when he started complaining about the women in his office, who turned into ball-breakers at the drop of a hat.

I stared blankly into space, not really listening to their chatter, and wondered why I had such a strong premonition of disaster. The motionless plane, which had only stopped pounding and shaking a few minutes ago, reminded me of a ship lifted high in the air on the crest of a wave. In my present mood, reading my book was out of the question, so I picked up the newspaper that was still in my lap and opened it with a snap to another page.

Meanwhile, the girl on the left: "You're either born with it or you're not, and that's *it!* We're a lot better at communicating than they are, that's a well-known fact. Nature has also given us ideal managerial qualities — a direct result of our maternal instincts. So I say, exploit your femininity, because if you don't, someone else will!" The girl on the right, musing: "At my office, we're always in for a bit of fun." The left: "Oh, at mine too!" The right: "Our policy is first and foremost physical. Why shouldn't you make a statement with your breasts? Or cash in on your womanhood? Last week I had a business meeting to discuss a pretty tough issue — my commission. So okay, the guy comes in, I shake hands, let him take a seat, turn around to pick up the proposal, catch him looking at my ass, and flash him a smile. Wow, what a power trip!" The left: "A couple of days ago I had to bone up on private banking, but I was in a hurry, or I was too lazy, or something. Anyway, I walked over to the documentation center and said to the sweet guy sitting there at his computer, 'Everyone has their limits.' He looked up, and I smiled, all honey and cream, and I'm wearing this wrap sweater, you know the one I mean. Well, he's a goner from the moment his hormones go into overdrive, so I confess to him that I'm not really good at surfing the Net and that maybe he, uh, wouldn't mind, uh . . ." The two girls burst into peals of laughter and one of them started quietly singing "I'm Climbing to the Top."

♪

I must have been staring at it for quite some time.

Actually, I no longer read the obituaries. I started skipping over those black-bordered notices a couple of years ago, when more and more of them contained the names of people I knew. It shocked me to note at a single glance that a human life had been snuffed out, reduced to a mere name.

Suzanna Flier.

My heart skipped a beat. I brought the paper closer to my face and stared, as in a dream, at the two words of the name until they were drained of all reality. Then I began to read the notice, with its old-fashioned obligatory start: "To our great sorrow . . ." And the facts began to sink in. Suzanna Flier, beloved wife and mother, had been killed in a fateful accident, a plane crash, which wasn't specified, but which I had read about a few days ago in the paper. She had apparently been traveling alone, or in any case not with her loved ones — the death notice listed four family members, all living in Wassenaar: Marius van Vlooten and the children Benno, Beatrijs, and Lidwien. Nor had she been traveling with the three other members of the Schulhoff Quartet, for they had placed their own expression of sympathy on the same page.

What was there to say?

The story was over. It left me in a state of shock and amazement. Events had not gone as I imagined, and after sixteen years I needed to readjust the picture of reality I had been carrying around in my head all this time. I looked up, caught sight of the approaching beverage cart, nodded at the flight attendant, and pointed, speechless, at the Scotch. It is said that there are no words to describe such situations, but I had two.

So they had been reconciled, I thought, and mentally toasted van Vlooten and Suzanna Flier. Splendid! Everything had turned out all right after all — who could have imagined that? — and during the years in which I had lost sight of them, I had forgotten that a pair of hearts had gone on beating, with warmth, longing, and, yes, even with a sense of beauty toward their very special case. Reconciled! I shook my head, quickly emptied my glass, and wondered what the next stop on this line would be, for I felt sure it would go on. Works of art have no respect for the dead, I thought tipsily. They use the known to assail the unknown, work it into their themes, then hand back these themes, in the form of blueprints, to real life. I looked once more at the list of names in the crumpled newspaper. Beatrijs and Lidwien … Thirteen- or fourteen-year-old girls, that's how I imagined them, daughters, maybe even twins, which Suzanna Flier had given birth to, much to her husband's delight.

"Another drink, sir?"

The flight attendant was already unscrewing the cap.

I drank, sitting perfectly still, my seat belt fastened. The accident had greatly stirred the public imagination, but because I had been working on my lectures, I had watched very little TV. The plane, on its way from New York to Brussels, had exploded off Long Island shortly after takeoff. Eyewitnesses, looking out at the ocean from their living rooms, had seen a ball of fire and, after the explosion, white smoke drifting toward the sea. Experts all agreed that the people on board didn't have the slightest chance when the cabin ripped apart, a gaping hole came racing toward them, and at 7,500 feet, the tail was transformed into a burning inferno as they rushed toward life's last, invariable plot.

With thanks to Henk Guittart, the viola player in the Schönberg Quartet, and Milan Škampa, the viola player in the Smetana Quartet, for their analysis of Janáček's String Quartet no. 1, which forms the basis of chapter 12.